A Further Stir of Porridge

D0785555

Dick Clement
and Ian La Frenais

A Further Stir of
PORRIDGE

adapted from the TV series
by Paul Victor

British Broadcasting Corporation

Published by the
British Broadcasting Corporation
35 Marylebone High Street
London W1M 4AA

ISBN 0 563 17214 2

First published 1977

© Dick Clement and Ian La Frenais 1977

Printed in England by
Love & Malcomson Ltd
Brighton Road, Redhill, Surrey

All characters in this book
are fictitious and any reference
to people living or dead
is coincidental

This book is sold subject to the condition that it
shall not, by way of trade or otherwise, be lent, re-sold,
hired out or otherwise circulated without the publisher's prior
consent in any form of binding or cover other than that in which
it is published and without a similar condition including this
condition being imposed on the subsequent purchaser.

Contents

The Desperate Hours

It was the night before Christmas and all through the nick, not a creature was stirring not even a tick. Which was not surprising because Slade Prison, while plentifully stocked with cockroaches, mice and screws, does not number any ticks amongst its vermin. To the best of my knowledge, that is. And my knowledge is pretty extensive since I have spent many years within its grand old walls. And if it burned down tomorrow I would not shed a tear. Assuming I was outside its grand old walls. Which is not a very sound assumption since I still have a long time to serve. Moreover, it was not really the night before Christmas which I just said to make the rhyme. Nevertheless, the season of turkey and plum pudding, represented inside by stringy bones and brown goo, was fast approaching. For this reason, and in an attempt to increase the meagre amount of merriment normally available to convicted felons, I had summoned a meeting in the conference hall, otherwise known as the latrines. I addressed the delegates.

'McLaren, Warren, Tulip, Godber, I have gathered you here as representatives of your respective cell blocks.'

'What's all this about, Fletch?' Bunny Warren asked.

'A minute, please. As you know, the festive season is almost upon us.'

'With all the high spirits and jollity which that entails,' McLaren growled.

'Now, come on, Jock, that's the wrong attitude, that is. Let me ask you all, what is the real meaning of Christmas?'

'Robbing postmen?' offered Tulip.

'Not the professional meaning. I mean, what comes to mind when you hear the word Christmas?'

'Chestnuts roasting on an open fire,' Lennie tried.

'Yeah, well – that is one thing.'

'How about MacKay roasting on an open fire?' McLaren suggested.

'Guy Fawkes night, that is,' I corrected him.

Warren wrinkled his tiny brow and then said : 'Crackers? Holly?'

Lennie carrolled : 'Treetops glistening and children listening to hear – '

'That will do, Godber. You can leave out the Perry Como. Look, I'm talking about what the likes of us associate with Christmas. There's one thing above all else which conjures up the very spirit of this joyous occasion.'

'What?' asked Tulip.

'Booze.'

'Eh?'

'Booze, you nurk. Drink. Juice. What does everyone do at Christmas? They get drunk. Bombed. Plastered. Elephant's trunk. Legless. Brahms and Liszt as the proverbial newt.'

Lennie confided to McLaren. 'I've never understood the derivation of that expression myself. Are newts known to be heavy drinkers?'

I held up an irritated hand. 'Time *is* somewhat precious. We are running a security risk.'

'Sorry, Fletch,' Lennie said apologetically.

'Right.'

'Well, what *are* we here for, Fletch?' asked Tulip.

I looked around at them with a proud look and then fed them the glad tidings.

'Wine tasting.'

Tulip goggled very satisfyingly. 'Wine tasting?'

'Yeah. Unbeknownst to all and sundry, and out of charity to our fellow inmates, young Godber and me have been fermenting illicit liquor since last July. We done this so it would reach its peak maturity at this festive season.'

McLaren shook his head in unashamed admiration. 'Fletch, you're a marvel. You're a naffing marvel, you know that?'

I lowered my eyes modestly. 'Yeah, well – '

Lennie said plaintively : 'I helped him as well.'

'And are you dishing the stuff out, like?' Warren asked eagerly.

'You mustn't take that word "charity" too literally, Bunny. This is a business transaction. You are here to obtain a free sample sip and then place orders for your fellow felons. Lennie?'

The lad trotted obediently to cubicle number two, stood on the seat and extracted from the cistern two different bottles of precious liquor.

'We are offering two selections,' I continued. 'We have the five star in the white bottle and two star in the blue bottle.'

At this moment, 'Tinker' Brown, who was minding, stuck his head in and said 'Oi!'. Lennie immediately slammed the door of his cubicle from the inside and the rest of us, like a well-drilled platoon, hit the urinals and stood in a convincing row with our hands in the appropriate position. A screw entered, prowled around for a minute or so and then, satisfied, departed again. The auction got back into swing.

'Now,' I continued, 'as I was saying, the two star is the van ordinairy, though I might say it ain't that ordinary. The five star is our special reserve. We'll sample that first.'

Lennie filled a bottle-cap with the colourless fluid. I

went on : 'I'd like to warn you, gentlemen, that this wine should be sipped delicately, like a fine liqueur. It should not be smashed down the throat by the mugfull. Right.'

I watched critically as the bottle-cap passed from hand to hand. Sheer delight seemed for a moment to rob the tasters of the power of speech. I said approvingly : 'I knew they'd like it, Len.'

Then Warren, surfacing with a strangled gasp, suggested : 'You should have washed the bottle out first.'

McLaren, in a faintly unnatural voice, wheezed : 'Fletcher, are you sure this stuff is fit for human consumption?'

'Candidly, I'm not. That's why I got you three nurks to test it for me.'

'This stuff's evil, Fletcher.'

'Yeah, but don't forget it's got another week to mature. Lennie, give them the two-star. I should warn you, gentlemen, that this one isn't quite so smooth. Be careful, otherwise not only will you lose the flavour and bouquet, you may lose the lining of your throat as well.'

McLaren raised the cap to his nose and sniffed. 'Smells like embrocation.'

I nodded. 'Just a hint of that, yes.'

Tulip protested : 'You could poison the whole prison, Fletcher.'

I sighed. 'It's not all that easy to get the right ingredients in here, you know. I got the potato peelings and the orange pips okay. No bother. But normally I would have avoided boot polish.'

As the howls of dismay broke out, I grinned and said quickly : 'Only a joke, only a joke.'

Warren, with the cap at his lips, asked suspiciously : 'Are you sure?'

'Of course I am,' I said firmly. Warren sipped, as I added : 'It was anti-freeze.'

Well, although the product was not quite up to the standard of the best malts, Lennie and I shifted a fair amount of it, naturally keeping a supply of the least vile batch for our own use. Now, of course, in the nick, making, or attempting to make, illicit hooch is a minor industry. Actually, the problem is not so much manufacturing the stuff as stashing it away where the screws won't find it once it's made. A good deal of ingenuity goes into this attempt. I remember a firm in A Block thought they'd found the answer with a fire extinguisher. They filled it with home-brew and inhaled a gulp from the nozzle whenever they went past. Everything was going fine until a fire broke out in the education room. It was only a small blaze but after the screws turned that particular extinguisher on it, it became a raging inferno. Still, Lennie and I felt we had found a solution to this ancient problem.

Now the Governor of Slade Prison is a strict teetotaller and hates drink worse than a bishop hates sin. He conducts unceasing war against it. For this reason we were not surprised when we returned to the old flowery a day or two later to find Barrowclough turning it over. We paused in the doorway.

'Hello, hello,' I muttered. 'I think we've got burglars.' Barrowclough turned his melancholy eye upon us. 'What's this then?' I asked.

'You're not being singled out, Fletcher. We're doing the whole block.'

'Harassment. Despicable infringement of civil liberties,' Lennie said contemptuously.

But I said politely: 'If you told us what you was looking for, Mr Barrowclough, we might be able to save you all this bother.'

He peered under the lower bunk and said: 'Drink.'

'Drink?' I asked in a shocked voice. 'You mean

alcohol? The demon rum? Mother's ruin?'

Barrowclough straightened himself up and glanced about forlornly. He looked like a cow that's been tethered just out of reach of a clump of juicy thistles.

'That's what I mean, yes.'

I shook my head. 'I'm a strict teetotaller, Mr Barrowclough.'

'Are you really, Fletcher?'

'Oh yes. Never touch tea, never have. You know something, Mr Barrowclough, the pathetic state of this country today has got more to do with tea than alcohol.'

'How do you reach that conclusion, Fletcher?'

'Because tea necessitated the tea-break and that's where the rot set in.'

'You're in no position to point the finger, Fletcher, when you've never done an honest day's work in your life.'

'Oh, that's very nice.' I appealed to Lennie. 'He's added slander now to breaking and entering.'

Lennie said indignantly : 'They've been at it all week. D'you know what they did last night? They come in the hobby shop, where we was making soft toys for orphan children, and with my own eyes I saw Mr Barrowclough disembowelling my panda.'

Barrowclough looked unhappy.

'Don't you think I felt bad about that? Just as I felt bad about sampling your food parcels.'

It was rumoured that Barrowclough had tasted a bit of Christmas cake and inadvertently devoured about three grammes of marihuana. I chuckled and said :

'I heard you felt pretty good afterwards, though.' I informed Lennie. 'They found him standing in a bucket of sand singing the Desert Song.'

Barrowclough blushed. 'Yes, well, I suggest you men get this cell tidied up.'

He hastened out and I said very loudly :

'Exit the red shadow. Charming. They don't find nothing but we get no apologies, no retraction. As you say, Len, a total infringement of civil liberties. An unjustifiable act of mistrust and suspicion.'

Lennie said softly : 'They didn't find nowt, though.'

I also lowered my voice. 'Course not, we hid it too well. Shut the door and fetch your mug.'

Lennie got his mug and I got mine. Then I stationed myself at the head of the bunks.

'Evening, sir,' I said. 'And what will it be?'

'The usual,' Lennie said.

'Large one?'

'Mind your own business.'

'Very good, sir.'

'And have one yourself.'

'Oh, thank you, sir.'

After this chaff, if that's the right word, I got down to business. I unscrewed a particular screw from the bedstead and – lo and cadabra ! – clear fluid gushed from the pipe-frame into Lennie's mug. It was a treat to see it. The screws poke and ferret and check and vet and spy and inspect and here, under their very noses, illicit hooch was gushing as from a sacred spring. I filled Lennie's mug and then my own. We raised these vessels, clinked them together and quaffed deep. When my scalp had landed again and the sound of cannon-fire had abated somewhat, I wheezed :

'Prisoners one, systems nil.'

But my blood, already chilled by contact with our home-brew, now froze into ice-cubes as a sinister voice behind me rasped :

'Not necessarily, Fletcher.'

I spun round, and then, possibly as a result of the fine properties of our poteen, continued spinning for a few revs. When I finally came to rest I saw what I had most dreaded : MacKay's face leering triumphantly at me. He'd got us bang to rights. I groaned :

'Oh my gawd – time, gentlemen, please ! Now then – ain't you got no cells to go to?'

Thus it came to pass that before many moons, or even minutes, had passed, MacKay was marching Len and me into the Governor's outer office.

'Left, right, halt, face the front. Good morning, Mrs Jamieson, Mr Barrowclough – '

The recipients of these cordial salutations were, in this order, seated at her desk, frowning at a requisition, and seated on a bench cradling a large, and doubtless contraband-containing, Christmas cake on his lap. They both returned MacKay's greetings. The atmosphere seemed friendly and, thus encouraged, I began :

'Good-morning, Mrs Jamieson, you're looking very – '

'Quiet, Fletcher!' barked MacKay, shattering the seasonable mood. He asked Barrowclough : 'Is the Governor in?'

'Well, I'm waiting to see him. He's indisposed.'

Mrs Jamieson elaborated :

'He's not feeling too well. It came on after he sampled the Christmas pudding.'

'Here, I made that,' Lennie exclaimed miffily. 'Nothing wrong with it.'

I commented :

'That's what you said about your Hungarian gluelash.'

'The word is goulash, Fletcher,' said MacKay.

'I chose the word advisedly, Mr MacKay, seeing as most of us were stuck in the bog.'

'Attention !' bellowed MacKay, and, as we snapped to it, Mr Venables, looking distinctly under-chuffed and definitely below par, tottered cautiously through the outer office towards his lair.

MacKay's countenance became wreathed in a servile smile as he addressed his chief.

'Morning, Governor.'

'Hm? Oh, good morning, Mr MacKay.'

'You're not feeling too good, I hear, sir. Very sorry.'

'Thank you, Mr MacKay. No, I'm not too good. Can't seem to settle down, if you understand me. Have to keep hurrying back and forth.' He turned to his charming secretary. 'I suppose I'd better have some more of that vile medicine, Mrs Jamieson, though it doesn't seem to have slowed me down at all so far. Right, Mr Barrowclough, you can come through, but I warn you I may not be able to stay long.'

The Governor reeled on into his inner office and Barrowclough, bearing his cake before him, followed. Mrs Jamieson produced a bottle of evil green fluid from a drawer in her desk and began pouring a tot for the Governor. I reproached Lennie.

'See what you've done? A stricken Governor. What sort of Christmas is he going to have?'

MacKay chuckled evilly.

'What sort of Christmas are you two going to have?'

I gave him a haughty glance.

'Chuffed, aren't you?' I asked.

'It's your own fault, Fletcher. You know the penalties for brewing illicit hooch.'

'That wasn't illicit hooch. It was a health drink.'

'Poppycock.'

'No, we couldn't get any poppies. Of course, there's no shortage of – '

'Fletcher!' he warned, with an apprehensive glance at Mrs Jamieson. She was still fiddling with the Governor's cocktail and didn't seem to have noticed that anything was amiss.

'I'm just saying, it was a health drink. Me and a few

15

hundred of the lads saved up a wine gum each. Then we crushed them in the press in the woodwork shop. The resultant extract is a remedy for all known ills.'

Lennie said enthusiastically: 'You should give the Governor some, Mrs Jamieson.'

But the lady responded with no more than a vague smile to Len's kindly suggestion. Then she took her finished preparation and tripped off into the Governor's office. Lennie and I naturally took the opportunity to inspect as much of her shapely lower limbs as became visible. This was not much but, to your imprisoned felon, even a lingering glance –

'Stop that, you two !' roared MacKay.

Lennie said wistfully, 'I've always been attracted to older women. When I was a lad, I always wanted to be seduced by my Auntie Pauline. She was very sophisticated. Worked in a dress shop in Smethwick and wore Evening in Paris behind her ears.'

I nodded sagely.

'Behind the ears, eh? Sure sign, that is.'

Lennie continued :

'I nearly was once.'

'Was what?'

'Seduced. I went round to her house and the radio was on and she said : "Lennie, it's time you learned how to do the foxtrot." Well, even at the naïve age of four-teen, I thought to myself : "Foxtrot? In the middle of the day? Yum, yum." '

I noticed that MacKay was all ears and I cautioned Lennie : 'Is this suitable for Mr MacKay, Len? He's Edinburgh Presbyterian, you know. Sex is only permitted when Hearts beat Celtic.'

MacKay snorted. 'I am not interested in Godber's carnal reminiscences.' He strode jerkily to a chair and sat down.

I said encouragingly : 'Well, I am. So what happened, Len?'

'Nothing.'

'What?'

'Nothing happened. I mean, she held me very close like, but for an hour we just danced round the living-room accompanied by the Northern Dance Orchestra.'

I sighed. 'Godber, your stories have a way of tailing off. You are the master of the anti-climax.'

'I can't half foxtrot though.'

At this point, two small incidents occurred to break the monotony. Mrs Jamieson returned from the Governor's inner office with an empty glass. She replaced it in her desk drawer and then sat down at the desk. A moment later, there was a knock at the outer door, and in came Reg Urwin, a con I knew slightly. Reg was wearing a red band on his arm and carrying a tray full of coffee and biscuits. He started slightly at seeing so many people and then muttered :

'Oh, hello, lads.'

I greeted him. 'Hello, Reg. Trusty now, are we?'

'Er, yes. Replaced Keegan, thanks to Mr MacKay.'

MacKay said piously : 'If a man keeps his nose clean, I don't forget.'

'What happened to Keegan, then?' I asked.

'The Governor had him replaced,' said Reg. 'He didn't like having a poisoner serving him his coffee.' He went on nervously : 'Should I come back later?'

'Not at all, lad,' said MacKay. 'Take the Governor his coffee. Chop, chop.'

Now for the remainder of this true-life saga, you may be surprised to find that I sometimes recount events that occurred simultaneously in the Governor's inner office and his outer office. Since I could not be in both places at once, you will wonder how I perform this feat. Moreover, for one crucial period I was, for reasons that will become clear, deep in slumber. And yet I propose to acquaint you with what was going on as I slept. How do I do it? Exactly the way your Fearless Crime Reporter does it. He spends his days pressing down the brass rail in the Fleet Street boozer. But informants come to him and tell him who's been knifing who. Then he writes it all up and gets the George Medal. I don't expect any George Medal for what's coming but I *can* vouch for its truthfulness, having checked the facts with Lennie, Barrowclough and some of the others who also lived through The Desperate Hours.

Reg Urwin, a mild-looking but somewhat distracted con, doing a very long sentence, passed on into the Governor's inner office. There he placed his tray down carefully on the Governor's desk and said humbly:

'Your coffee, sir.'

'Oh, thank you, er – '

'That's right, Urwin, sir. With a "U". I'm the new trusty.'

'That's a privileged position, Urwin.'

'I know it is, sir. That's why I've been so well-behaved the last few months. So that I could get this job and then get on with my plan.'

Venables, who had been listening in mild surprise, suddenly clutched his stomach and registered anguish. He leapt to his feet, remarking: 'I'm afraid your plan will have to wait, Urwin.'

Then he made a dash for the door. This left Urwin and Barrowclough together in the Governor's inner office. Urwin gazed after the fleeing Governor with some displeasure.

'Where's he gone?'

Barrowclough explained. 'He has a bit of an upset tummy.'

'But he was instrumental in my plan, he was,' Reg said peevishly.

'What plan is this, Urwin?'

Whereupon Reg, thinking aloud as it were, muttered: 'I suppose a screw's just as good. Yeah, I don't see why not.'

Barrowclough, now distinctly uneasy, asked more firmly: 'I said, what is your plan?'

'I want to get out of here.'

'That's what we all want, Urwin.'

'Yes, but you don't want me to get out as soon as what I do. That's why I'm taking you hostage.'

With which, Reg produced from inside his working denims a crude and obviously home-made, but still dangerous-looking, gun. This he pointed at Barrowclough who favoured the weapon with an incredulous stare. Reg explained:

'It's a gun. And it works. And it's loaded.'

Barrowclough recoiled slightly and said, 'Now, just a moment, eh – '

'Urwin – with a "U".'

'Now, Urwin, why don't you put that gun down?'

'What, so you can pick it up?'

Barrowclough gulped. 'You should think very carefully about what you're doing.'

Urwin confided: 'Oh, I have done. Endless planning. Now here's what I want you to do. First, draw them blinds. Second, get me a helicopter.'

Mr Barrowclough merely gaped causing Reg to wave his pistol irritably and urge: 'Well, get on with it!'

Meanwhile, in the outer office, I was trying it on with MacKay.

'Listen,' I urged, 'the Governor's obviously got other things on his mind. So why don't we all come back in the New Year, Mr MacKay, say around April?'

MacKay chuckled out of the corner of his mouth as if afraid that, if he opened it fully, one of us would nick his teeth.

'Fletcher, I'm in no hurry. I've waited a long time for this moment.'

'In that case,' I said resignedly, 'let's take a seat.' With which Lennie and I lowered ourselves to the bench.

MacKay, inhibited by the presence of a lady from unleashing his full bellow, uttered a strangled protest. 'Fletcher, how dare you?'

'I don't mind waiting,' Lennie piped up cheerfully. 'It's almost worth getting busted these days, just for a glimpse of Mrs Jamieson's lovely – '

'Godber!' roared MacKay.

'Smile,' concluded Lennie meekly.

MacKay hastened towards the lady. 'I apologise for these two.'

But Mrs Jamieson was serene and composed. 'That's all right, Mr MacKay. Working in prison I've learned to turn the other cheek.'

'And a very attractive cheek, too,' Lennie offered.

At this point, a new diversion occurred to break the monotony. The connecting door opened and Mr Barrowclough poked a strange pale face through it. He smiled nervously and then addressed the secretary.

'Er – Mrs Jamieson, could you get in touch with the nearest RAF station?'

The good lady gave him a puzzled look and confessed : 'I'm afraid I don't know where it is.'

'Well, the Fleet Air Arm or the Air-Sea Rescue people. The thing is, I want a helicopter.'

'Being a bit lavish with your Christmas presents, aren't you, Mr Barrowclough?' I asked cheerfully.

He favoured me with a distracted glance.

'What?'

'You'll need a lot of coloured paper to wrap that up.'

But MacKay, every inch a screw, had sensed that something was up. 'Quiet, Fletcher,' he snapped, turning to his colleague. 'Is there a problem, Mr Barrowclough?'

'Yes, Mr MacKay, something's come up.'

'Come up?'

'Yes. I'm being held at gunpoint by Urwin here.' And he gestured over his shoulder.

MacKay bridled like an outraged turkey. 'You're what?' he goggled.

Whereupon Urwin materialised behind Barrowclough, waving his handiwork. 'It's true, look.'

Mrs Jamieson uttered a faint cry, whereupon Reg bent solicitous eyes upon her. 'Don't panic, missis. Just get on the blower.'

I sighed deeply and shook my head. 'Reg, have you gone off your rocker?'

'Shut up, Fletch.'

Discretion clearly being preferable to valour at this stage, I said soothingly, 'As you say, my son.'

MacKay, never the man to be intimidated by another's peril, started to advance on the mutinous felon. 'All right, Urwin, give me that gun.'

'You make a move and Barrowclough gets it,' Urwin warned.

MacKay stopped moving but continued to bluster : 'I said, give me that gun.'

'Do shut up, MacKay,' Barrowclough wailed. 'This is no time for stupid heroics.'

'We can't let these people intimidate us.'

'That's all very well for you to say, but it's my head the gun is pointing at.'

Urwin said, 'You just naff off out of here, MacKay. I've got two hostages – him and her – so you go and put the word out, right?'

MacKay squinted at Mrs Jamieson and then at Barrowclough.

'Do as he says, man!' urged Barrowclough.

MacKay finally sighed and nodded. He moved towards the outer door.

'Very well,' he agreed. 'Now, don't panic, Mrs Jamieson, soon have you out of this. And don't you panic, Mr Barrowclough.'

'Can we panic, Mr MacKay?' I asked.

'You two come along with me,' he said firmly.

But Urwin didn't take to this scheme. He exclaimed: 'No. They stay. I can use them. Now naff off, MacKay.'

Whereupon MacKay slipped out of the office and our long ordeal began.

Mrs Jamieson, who had been consulting the phone book, announced: 'I've found the number for RAF Topcliff.'

'Get them then,' Urwin ordered.

She started to dial. Lennie and I exchanged a glance and then I addressed Urwin winningly.

'Listen, Reg, you don't really need us. We're only littering up the place. We'll just be getting back to our cell if it's all the same to you. Busy day ahead.'

But Reg wasn't having any. He waved his do-it-yourself shooter.

'No, I need you two. Lock that door, Godber.' Lennie naturally obeyed. 'Now both of you, move that filing cabinet up against it.'

We started to comply. Mrs Jamieson said: 'I have them on the line, Mr Barrowclough.'

Barrowclough, nervous as a heifer before the cattle show, asked: 'Er – should I – talk to them in the inner office?'

Urwin nodded. 'Yeah, go on.'

Whereupon Barrowclough eased himself through into

the Governor's den while Reg lounged in the doorway, covering both rooms.

'Is that all you wanted us for, Reg?' Lennie asked. 'To move the cabinet?'

'Yeah.'

'Right, well that's done. So we'll just be moseying along then.'

'Let's get this shifted, Len,' I said quickly. And we started to move the filing cabinet away from the door again but Reg, although far from top heavy, perceived something was wrong.

'Hey! Think I'm crackers or something?'

We abandoned the cabinet. I shook my head sadly. 'It *is* possible, Reg. Your behaviour ain't exactly that of a rational man.'

He said stoutly, 'I know what I'm doing. Give me that key. Now, we'll just sit tight and wait.'

Mrs Jamieson remarked: 'I have a dental appointment in half an hour.'

'Then you'll have to bleeding cancel it,' Urwin said impatiently.

Meanwhile, in the inner office Barrowclough had established contact with RAF Topcliff.

'Hello? Yes, this is Prison Officer Barrowclough of Slade Prison and I'd like to speak to your commanding officer. What's that, Flight Sergeant? I realise there's only two shopping days left to Christmas but this happens to be a matter of some urgency.'

Urwin seized the phone from Barrowclough's moist hand.

'Listen here,' he began unceremoniously, 'this is Reg Urwin with a "U". I'm in charge. I've got the gun. I'm holding a man and a woman as hostages. Now, I don't care how you do it, but I want a chopper here in half an hour. And – don't go away. I also want ten thousand quid in used notes. Otherwise I'm not responsible for my actions.' With which persuasive offer, he slammed down the phone and remarked to Barrowclough : 'That's the way to talk to those people. If they ring back and they're still stalling, make believe I'm going to kill you.'

'I'll try to remember that,' quavered Barrowclough.

On our side of the door, Lennie approached Mrs Jamieson. 'Bearing up?'

'Pardon?'

'Under the strain, like.'

'Oh, I'm keeping myself busy. I'm doing those little jobs one's always putting off. Helps keep my mind occupied so that I don't go to pieces.'

'Oh, not you, Mrs Jamieson. I think you're holding up extremely well. Typically British, if I may say so. Stiff upper lip. Calm under crisis and all that sort of thing.'

Mrs Jamieson beamed. 'How sweet of you to say so.'

'To be quite honest, it doesn't surprise me. I've always admired you, Mrs Jamieson. From afar, like.'

'Really? Why?'

'You remind me of my Auntie Pauline.'

'Horny little beast,' I murmured.

'He was just trying to keep my spirits up,' Mrs Jamieson protested.

There was a knock at the outer door. Without thinking, I called : 'Come in. Oh, of course, you can't, can you? Give us a hand to shift this, Lennie.'

Urwin darted in from the Governor's sanctum.

'Here, wait a minute, wait a minute, who is it?'

I transmitted this message, bawling through the door : 'Wait a minute, wait a minute, who is it?'

'It's Mr MacKay. I've brought the coffee you asked for.'

I passed this on to Reg. 'It's Mr MacKay with the coffee we asked for.'

It occurred to me that I had no recollection of any coffee having been requested but Reg, who, as I said, is not a front-runner in the IQ stakes, failed to sniff any rats.

'All right,' he said, 'let him in – but watch it.'

I shouted, 'All right, you can come in. But watch it.'

Lennie and I shifted the naffing filing cabinet once more and opened the door with the key which Reg had handed over. MacKay stood there with a tray, looking like the head waiter in a doss house. He handed over the delicious and, I strongly suspected, doctored fluid and then glanced quickly about to see if bodies littered the floor.

'Is everything all right in there, Fletcher?' he asked.

But Reg, brandishing his improvised cannon, stormed forwards. 'Everything's all right. So naff off, MacKay.'

MacKay, pulling back, remarked, 'I can't believe a thing like this is happening in my prison. And at Christmas.'

I said sardonically : 'It's all right for you lot out there. Just remember it's us what are going through this terrifying ordeal.'

'That'll do, Fletch,' Urwin commanded. 'Lock the door, give me the key and put the cabinet back.'

As I began to comply, I whispered : 'Mr MacKay, one last thing. Could you do me a favour?'

He frowned and hissed back : 'What is it, Fletcher?'

'I left my socks soaking in the basin. Could you wring them out for me?'

And I pushed the door shut on his outraged gasp. Then Lennie and I battened down the hatches again and returned the key to Reg. He took it and went back into the inner office to have some coffee. When he got there, he found that Barrowclough had already poured it out into the mugs provided.

'Here we are, Urwin,' said the tense screw, handing over a mug.

'Ta,' grunted Urwin, taking the mug and quaffing deep.

Lennie and I entered respectfully.

'Fletcher, Godber,' invited Barrowclough, 'take a mug and help yourselves to sugar.'

We helped ourselves and I retreated with the treat to a retreat by the fireplace.

'Well, I must say, this is nice – very nice,' I observed. 'Never thought I'd be given coffee by a screw.'

'In the Governor's office, too,' Lennie added.

Barrowclough shook his head.

'Barriers tend to come down in situations like this.'

'You don't mind if I sit, then?'

'Go ahead,' said Reg.

I seated myself and took a swig. 'Here's to you, Reg. Wherever you ends up.'

Lennie asked : 'Where will you go, Reg?'

'Somewhere a long way away where they don't ask too many questions and don't care who I am as long as I can pay for it.'

'You mean somewhere corrupt where they turn a blind eye if you grease their palm?'

'Like,' I suggested, 'the Isle of Wight?'

Reg mused. 'I was thinking of South America or Mexico – somewhere like that.'

I nodded. 'Oh yeah, funny country, Mexico. Very Mexican. Apparently all the dogs limp.'

Mrs Jamieson looked surprised. 'I didn't know that.'

'Oh yes, well-known fact. Something to do with the food.'

'Food?' Lennie asked sceptically.

'Right. Bloke gets up in the morning, contemplates his horrible breakfast, and kicks the dog.'

Reg frowned, not certain as to how to take this information. 'Really?' he asked. 'I'd always rather fancied Mexico.'

I shook my head. 'No. Contrary to travel brochure myth, they're not a happy people. I suppose any country which has tequila as its national drink is bent on self-destruction.'

Reg nodded, as he finished his cup of coffee. 'I appreciate your advice, Fletch. Maybe I'll think of somewhere else.'

At this point, Barrowclough exclaimed : 'You won't be going anywhere, Urwin.'

Reg jumped and swung round with his Peacemaker. 'What?'

Barrowclough smiled with what seemed on the face of it unlikely confidence. He seized Urwin's empty mug and flourished it.

'Don't you think we have well-rehearsed precautions for emergencies like this? Don't you worry, Mrs Jamieson, you and I will not be going South of the Border down Mexico way today.'

Reg glanced about uneasily. 'What you on about?'

Barrowclough bored on.

'Didn't it puzzle you that I was being so polite, handing out the coffee? That was because one of those mugs was laced with a powerful tranquilliser which acts very swiftly, and in a few moments, Urwin, in a few moments you will be happily asleep in the land of nod.'

This was, of course, exactly what I had anticipated. As if in confirmation of Mr Barrowclough's promise, a loud snore echoed round the room. I smiled. But a moment later, I opened my eyes with a jerk and gazed at Barrowclough in fury. The snore had issued from my own mouth ! The blundering nurk had only mixed up the –
my eyes sagged shut again. I passed out.

Meanwhile, an anxious conference was in progress outside the main door. Venables, who had just arrived, asked MacKay : 'Any word yet?'

'Not yet, no sir. But everything's under control. The rest of the prison is quiet. All the cells are locked. Cup of tea, sir?'

'No, no. So the men have no idea what's going on?'

'They know something's up. They probably think someone's gone over the wall.'

'We must keep the lid on this thing.'

MacKay glanced at his watch. 'That stuff should have worked by now. I put enough in to knock out a rhinoceros.'

Venables moaned : 'I still can't believe this is happening here. Where did he get the gun?'

'Probably made it. He's spent a lot of time in the machine shop has Urwin, and now one can see why.'

The phone rang. MacKay leapt upon it eagerly.

'Hello? Mr Barrowclough? Is everything – oh, Urwin! Yes – sorry – I meant – *Mr* Urwin. Yes, I – very well. Yes, I'll remember that.'

Grinding his teeth in impotent fury, MacKay replaced the phone. Venables demanded : 'What's happened?'

'Urwin says thank you for the coffee. It perked him up. Fletcher, on the other hand, is sleeping like a rhinoceros.'

In the inner office, where I was slumped unconscious, the phone rang. Mrs Jamieson answered it.

'Hello? Oh – just one moment.'

Urwin darted eagerly through the door. 'Is that for me?'

'I'm afraid not.' Mrs Jamieson rose demurely and proceeded to the connecting door. She addressed the captive screw. 'It's your wife, Mr Barrowclough.'

The news seemed to do nothing to ease the poor fellow's burden. 'Oh dear,' he gulped. 'How does she sound?'

'Same as usual.'

Barrowclough repeated: 'Oh dear.' He asked Urwin, 'May I?'

'Be my guest.'

Barrowclough went to the telephone. 'Hello, dear? What? No, I haven't forgotten but I think I should tell you there's a chance I may be late this evening ... Now, just a minute, Alice ... Alice, if you'd give me a moment to explain – I know I've been late three times this week already, but I'm being held at gunpoint as a hostage ... Yes, I know we're supposed to visit Mrs Wainwright at eight ... Yes, I admit it's rude and inconsiderate, but I may be going abroad in a helicopter ... Alice, will you please pay attention – yes, I did say at gunpoint ... Who? Well, there's Mrs Jamieson, two prisoners and myself ... What do you mean, "Is that woman going with you?" Of course she's going too. We've neither of us got much choice. Of course I'm not delighted. Oh, look, this is pointless. I'll try and call later but if I don't I suggest you watch the six o'clock news.'

Urwin, although not blessed with a razor intellect, had noticed that, during this conversation, Mrs Jamieson had turned pink and retreated into the outer office. He grinned at poor Barrowclough.

'So your old lady reckons you and Mrs Jamieson have got a little thing going, eh, Barra?'

Barrowclough said firmly, but with a giveaway glance in the lady's direction, 'Certainly not.'

Urwin grinned lewdly. 'I bet she don't believe you've been working all these late shifts.'

Lennie said judiciously, 'Now, Reg, this thing going between Mr Barrowclough and Mrs Jamieson is sheer speculation.'

Barrowclough protested. 'There is no "thing", Godber. Our relationship is purely professional.'

Mrs Jamieson entered briskly and began clearing the desk. She remarked, 'I'll just take these cups out, Mr Barrowclough.'

Reg grinned. 'No need to be so formal with him, love. We know all about you two.'

Mrs Jamieson dropped a mug and turned fiercely on poor Barrowclough. 'Henry! How could you!'

'Dorothy, I never said a word.'

'Well, it certainly never came from my lips.'

And she turned and stormed out of the inner office. As she did so, she inadvertently gave me a light kick on the ankle and this, together with the fact that I have a powerful constitution and was in a very uncomfortable position, was enough to restore a glimmer of consciousness. My eyes flickered open.

'Where am I?' I murmured.

I heard Lennie's voice somewhere a long way off. 'We're in the Governor's office, remember, Fletcher?'

I rose swaying to my feet and saluted. I mumbled: 'Oh yes, sir, about Mr MacKay's allegations. Godber and me weren't drunk. We never drink. I admit we chew the occasional sock but – '

It became difficult to continue because I found I was swaying like a sapling in the breeze. I focused with care and found that Lennie was shaking me.

'Fletch, Fletch – the Governor isn't here. Don't you remember?' And he jerked a finger towards a figure in the middle distance. I readjusted my vision and someone I knew slightly swam into sight.

'Hello, Reg,' I greeted him. 'Are you the new Governor?'

He smiled. 'So you're awake again, Fletch. I'm hijacking Barrowclough.'

'Oh yes? How could I have nodded off and missed all the fun?'

Barrowclough explained glumly: 'The coffee you drank was drugged.'

'Drugged?'

'It was meant for Reg, but Barrowclough mucked it up,' Lennie amplified.

I became aware that my stomach seemed to be trying to do a knees-up and I sagged back in the chair. 'I do feel a bit queer.'

'Could be dangerous, Fletch,' said Lennie helpfully. 'Those drugs on top of all the booze we had.'

Barrowclough turned on us. 'Thank you, Godber, I'll remember that.'

Before I could say anything, Mrs Jamieson tripped in with a transistor radio. 'Listen, we're on "The World at One",' she said excitedly.

A tinny voice came from the tiny set:

'A government spokesman said that the Home Secretary could not be reached for comment regarding the situation at Slade Prison. Details are still confused, but it appears that the Governor's secretary, Mrs Dorothy Jamieson' – at which the good lady blushed with pleasure and lowered her eyes modestly – 'and a prison officer are being held at gunpoint by three desperate prisoners –'

I rose to protest indignantly, felt my stomach make an attempt on the Olympic high-jump record, and sank down again. The ignorant nurk continued: 'They are demanding transportation and a large sum of money. In the City today, shares –'

Urwin clicked the set into silence.

'What's this about *three* desperate men?' I managed to say.

Barrowclough said soothingly: 'They said that details were confused.'

'And the next thing you know, they'll be issuing names.'

'What's my family going to think?' Lennie said in an aggrieved voice.

'What's my wife going to think?' I added.

'I only hope,' sighed Barrowclough, 'that she shows a little more consideration than mine.'

But just then Urwin, who had been frowning in quite a good imitation of a man deep in thought, exclaimed: 'Hey, hey, hey! Never mind your naffing families. What about me? It's on the wireless so everybody knows about it. So why am I still stuck here? Where's my helicopter?'

Reg seemed to be getting a trifle het up. Sick as I was, I knew that someone would have to calm him down and no one else seemed either willing or able. I rose unsteadily to my feet.

'Here, Reg, a word of caution. Don't build your hopes too high, my son.'

'What d'you mean?'

'Well, I think you should get used to the idea that they may not play ball. I mean, put yourself in their shoes. They have to demonstrate to an anxious public that they ain't going to bow down to every nutter with a gun and fly him off to sunnier climes.'

I was aware that this speech was not up to the loftiest standards of diplomacy but then how would Kissinger make out if he had to bring about world peace with a skinful of home-brew and tranquillisers? Reg sputtered indignantly: 'Here! I'm no nutter.'

I said soothingly: 'I'm just taking the Establishment viewpoint, Reg. Nothing personal, you understand.'

'Another thing,' Lennie pointed out. 'Ten thousand is a lot of money, Reg.'

'Doesn't seem an excessive amount for a prison officer with twenty-three years of unblemished service,' Barrowclough said bitterly.

Reg began to get my drift. He said nervously: 'Let me

get this straight. What you're saying like is they're calling my bluff? They haven't been taking me seriously?'

Barrowclough, unwisely in my opinion, declared: 'That's right, Urwin. And there's nothing you can do about it.'

Reg was not in agreement. He remarked: 'There *is* one thing I could do.'

'What?'

Reg levelled his shooter at the dismayed screw. 'I could shoot you.'

Barrowclough seemed to perceive the force of this. He gulped: 'Yes, yes, I suppose you could do that.'

I commented, with what I hoped was just the right amount of emphasis: 'Wouldn't advise it, Reg. Any wave of public sympathy you might be attracting would go right out of the window if you was to maim a screw.'

Lennie supported me. 'You should listen to Fletch, Reg, and just keep cool.'

I pressed on. 'That's the ticket, son. Because I have been through this before, you see.'

'Have you?' Reg asked doubtfully.

Barrowclough gave me a sceptical look. Then, as much to gain time as anything, I spun them a yarn.

'Yeah. First nick I was in. There was this bloke Popplewell. He was a trusty like you, Reg. That's how he come to be on an outside work party. Repainting the Governor's house. Well, the next thing we knew he was barricaded in there with Mrs Bailey.'

'Mrs Bailey?' asked Barrowclough wonderingly, as if I'd said "Mrs Stalin".

'Yeah. Mrs Bailey, the Governor's wife. That was her name. It's a difficult tale I admit but try to follow it. The Governor's name was Bailey and this lady was married to him, so she was Mrs Bailey. All straightened out now?'

Lennie asked brightly: 'Was the Governor known as Old Bailey?'

I sighed. 'Do you want to tell this story, Godber?'

'I'm sorry, Fletch.'

'Yeah, well – '

'Please go on, Fletch.'

'Don't know if I can now. I've lost the thread.'

But Urwin was apparently on the edge of his seat. He pointed his Mauser and urged: 'Get on with it.'

'All right, all right. Well now, before you could say Jack the Ripper the house was surrounded by the screws, and the bogies, and of course there was newspapers and television cameras. If I remember rightly, even Fyfe Robertson turned up. Anyhow, for three days all sorts of people made appeals to Popplewell – the Governor, the Chaplain and the psychiatrist. But there was never a word from either him or Mrs Bailey. You remember Mrs Bailey, Mr Barrowclough?'

'All right, Fletcher. What happened?'

'What happened? On the fourth day Mrs Bailey released him.'

Like I said, Reg would be unlikely to get the point of a joke if it poked his eye out, but I *was* disappointed with Lennie and Barrowclough. They just stared at me blankly.

'You seem to be implying that *she* was holding *him*. Why was that, Fletch?' Lennie asked.

I sighed and admitted: 'Well, to use a catchphrase what was prevalent at the time, she'd never had it so good.'

And my effort had done some good, too. Reg seemed a bit further from flash-point. He sat down and gazed accusingly at the telephone. And we sat and gazed at Reg.

Some twenty minutes later, I nudged Lennie. I rose and ambled into the outer office. He followed me.

'You all right, Mrs Jamieson?' I asked the lady when we got there.

She nodded and then inquired: 'What's happening in there?'

Lennie informed her. 'We've won a small victory. He's extended his deadline till five o'clock.'

We all looked at the big wall-clock. It said half-past four. Mrs Jamieson said briskly: 'That's good. Then I'll probably have time to finish this filing before he shoots us all. Or must I expect a fate worse than death?'

'Is there a fate worse than death?' I grunted.

Mrs Jamieson considered this for a moment. Then shook her head. 'No, I don't suppose there is.'

I glanced at the dividing door, lowered my voice and asked her: 'Are these the prisoners' files? In this cabinet?'

'Yes.'

'Just fish Urwin's out for me, would you?'

'Why?'

'Might be useful. Never know. Have a quick shifty, Len. I'll go and distract Al Capone.'

I ambled back into the inner office as Lennie and Mrs Jamieson began rummaging through the files.

As I entered, Urwin looked up and said wildly: 'Listen, I'm getting bloody angry now. When are we going to get some action around here?'

Barrowclough said quickly: 'I'm still waiting to hear from the Governor, as you know.'

'Well, I can't wait much longer. Just remember that.'

It was clearly time for me to have another go at shuttle diplomacy. I said earnestly, 'Reg, you seem kind of tense.'

He shook his head. He looked desperate. 'I got to get out, Fletch. Can't take any more.'

Barrowclough moaned: 'That's exactly how I feel.'

Reg swung round on him. 'You feel like that after half a day. I've been in stir half me life.'

Barrowclough tried to sound reasonable. 'But you're up for parole soon, Urwin.'

'They won't give it to me. Not a snowball's. They never have and they never will. And I just got to get out of here.'

'But why this way, Reg?' I asked.

'Because if I stay inside much longer, I'm going to top myself.'

'Suicide? You wouldn't do that, would you?'

'I tried it once before.'

I asked, trying to keep the tone conversational: 'Oh yes? How'd you make out?'

'I failed, didn't I? Typical. I was in a supermarket, trying to steal a tin of pork luncheon meat. Suddenly I thought: 'Is this what my life has come to? Stealing luncheon meat?'

'You tried to kill yourself in a supermarket? How?'

'I just put me head down and charged towards the glass doors.'

'And what went wrong?'

'They was electric. I ran head first into an off-duty cop. He booked me for nicking a tin of pork luncheon meat.'

I shook my head sadly. 'There's always one about when you don't need one. What you should realise, Reg, is you're one of those people who just doesn't get the breaks. Not even with glass doors. Today's typical. Obviously you've been planning to hijack the Governor for months. And the day you choose, he gets the runs.'

Just then I noticed Lennie in the doorway. He beckoned. Reg was deep in despair and did not notice me amble out again.

Lennie seemed quite excited. He handed me a file and urged: 'Just read that, Fletch.'

I began to do so. Lennie explained: 'Three times in

the past two years Urwin's been recommended for psychiatric treatment.'

I nodded grimly. 'And he never got it, did he? Well, it's the system what did this to Reg. I'll have to talk to him. Mrs Jamieson, would you come through here a minute, please?'

I led her through to the inner office where I requested: 'Sit down, love.' Then I turned to Urwin. 'Reg, can you come through and have a word with me and Godber? Private like?'

He seemed a bit uneasy about it. 'I dunno.'

'Come on, Reg,' said Lennie. 'These two can't get up to nowt. Well, maybe they can, but I don't think they'd want to with us in the next room.'

Urwin sighed. 'Okay then.'

Lennie dropped the file in front of Barrowclough and whispered: 'Read this – it should interest you.' Then he followed Reg and me back into the outer office.

I said: 'Here, Reg, sit down. You trust me, don't you?'

'Maybe.'

But he sat down. I said earnestly: 'Well, I've got to tell you, son. You ain't going to make it.'

He returned sadly: 'Got to make it, Fletch. I'm a three-time loser.'

I shook my head. 'I swear to you, there ain't no way. They got all the arguments on their side. Worst thing that could happen is if they say O.K. Because you know you'd never make it to that helicopter. They've got blokes out there could shoot a fly's eyebrows off at four hundred yards. Know what I mean? And say you got to Mexico. Where next? Look at you. You think you're going to check in to the Acapulco Hilton looking like that?'

Lennie, not very helpfully, contributed: 'They'd never let you in without a tie.'

I bent over Reg in a fatherly way. 'Reg, me and the

lad could have jumped you over the last few hours. But we didn't. You know why?'

'Why?'

'Because that would have dropped you in even further than what you is now. They have to see that you chucked in the towel yourself. Voluntary, like. Look, I won't lie to you. They're going to throw the book at you. But I've been reading your file. You've got some kind of case – but only if you give yourself up.'

He shifted uneasily. Then he shook his head. 'No, Fletch. I'm going through with it.'

'Think, Reg!'

'No!' He stood up. 'I'm going the distance.'

I sighed deeply, squared my shoulders and planted myself in front of him. 'In that case, you leaves me no choice. I'm going to have to take that gun off of you.'

He gaped. 'You're what?'

He backed away, brandishing the weapon. I said quietly : 'Give me the gun, Reg.'

I closed in on him slowly. I could see, out of the corner of my eye, Lennie goggling in amazement.

Urwin shouted : 'Stay where you are, Fletch.'

I shook my head. 'Reg, you're my mucker. You ain't going to shoot me.'

He aimed the gun, straight at my heart. 'Don't bank on it.'

Lennie said urgently : 'Hey, Fletch, give over! He's serious.'

But I kept advancing. 'Not to worry. Reg and me is mates.'

'Don't push it, mate,' suggested Reg.

I was only a couple of feet from him now. Very slowly I raised my hand – and pushed my finger up the barrel of his home-made gun. Reg gazed at me in anguish. I reached out my other hand and took the weapon from him. He collapsed in a chair, a beaten man. I put my arm round him.

'Now, Reg, on your feet, son. Don't let go. Now's the time you have to be in control.'

'What's the point?' he moaned.

'Every point. Mustn't let Barra think we overcame you. You go in there and tell him this was your decision. And Len and me will back you up.'

'He's right, Reg,' said Lennie. 'It's your only chance.'

Urwin glanced at us dubiously. 'You'd back me up?'

I assured him. 'Course we will. Like I said, we're still on the side of us. There's still them and us.'

Reg shook his head. 'But you two could be heroes. For what you two have just done, you could probably get a free pardon.'

At the words, my brain whirled. He was probably right and all. To march out of Slade Nick, get a train to London, spend Christmas with the family and – I looked at Lennie. From the faraway look on his face, I could see that similar pictures were floating before his eyes.

'What d'you think, Len?'

He sighed and shrugged. 'It is Christmas, after all.'

'Good will to all men and all that swaddling? Yeah.' I turned to Reg. 'On your way, son.'

He nodded. 'Maybe you're right, Fletch. Maybe this is the best way. But I'm still calling the shots, aren't I?'

As he got to his feet and started towards the door, I assured him : 'Course you are, Reg. Main thing is, you didn't shoot the shots.'

He opened the door and went into the other room. 'Mr Barrowclough – ' The door closed after him.

Lennie looked at me. 'Fletch, you are a ruddy marvel. I've never seen anything like it.'

He was gazing at me, his eyes alight with hero worship. It was a very satisfying moment.

'Oh – the gun, you mean? Well, that wasn't really – '

Lennie cut me off. 'No, don't denigrate what you just done. I never see anything like it. Not even in *Kojak*.'

I took up Reg's home-made pistol and weighed it in my hand. Gratifying though it was to have Godber treating me like a mixture of Wild Bill Hickock and Solomon, I knew it wouldn't survive an official examination of the evidence. I sighed and confessed:

'Yeah, well I had an advantage over Lollipop head, didn't I? I knew the gun weren't loaded.'

'Wasn't it?' asked Lennie wonderingly.

'No. I been working in the machine shop with Reg. He's been making that gun for months. It's only a toy.'

Lennie took the gun from me and peered at it. 'You knew that all along?'

'Yes, but as I just said, if I'd mentioned it, I'd have dropped him deeper in the clarts.'

I took the gun back. Lennie shook his head and remarked: 'It looks very authentic to me. Are you sure it's a toy?'

I nodded. 'Course I am. Look.'

I pointed the imitation toy pistol at the ceiling and pulled the trigger. There was a bang like Big Bertha going off and about half the ceiling clattered down on our heads. I damn near fainted.

That evening, I was putting up a paper chain in the cosy dell when Barrowclough strolled in.

'Evening, Fletcher,' he said cordially.

'Oh, hello, Mr Barrowclough.'

He studied the paper chain. 'This is very nice. Is Godber about?'

'No, he wanted to prove that his Christmas pudding was not the cause of the Governor's indisposition. So he ate three helpings to vindicate his reputation.'

'I see. And where is he then?'

'In the bog.'

'Poor lad. And how are you feeling after our terrible ordeal?'

'I'm all right, Mr Barrowclough. But me and the lads are still a bit concerned about Reg Urwin.' I pulled a chair to the right spot, got up on it and added a new bit of paper chain.

'I have been assured that Urwin will be undergoing psychiatric treatment. He will not be punished so much as helped.'

'Yeah – well – not before time.'

'And I had a word with the Governor and in appreciation of your conduct the charges against you and Godber will be dropped.'

I got down from the chair. 'Charges? Oh, you mean those unfounded allegations about us making booze? Well, that's only right and proper, that is.'

'Enough said, Fletcher.'

'Yeah, but we don't get our booze back, do we?'

Barrowclough seemed uneasy as if there was something else on his mind which he was finding difficulty in mentioning. I tried to help.

'Something bothering you, Mr Barrowclough?'

'What? No, certainly not – nothing at all, except possibly that I would like to think that you could forget certain things that may have been revealed during those desperate hours.'

I contemplated the paper chain. It wasn't hanging right. I got up on the chair again. 'Like what?'

'Well, th – er – the rather delicate matter of Mrs Jamieson and myself. I'd like it to go no further.'

I said innocently : 'No idea what you're on about, Mr Barrowclough.'

I descended once more to cell level. Barrowclough seemed chuffed. 'That's the spirit, Fletcher.'

'If you're trying to tell me there's something I'm supposed to forget, I think you're overlooking the fact that I was asleep most of the time. Didn't hear a thing.'

Barrowclough's jaw dropped. I half expected a cud to fall out.

'You mean – you didn't know about myself and Mrs Jamieson?'

'No, sir, I didn't. But don't worry – I do now, Henry.'

A Storm in a Teacup

What's *your* idea of life in the nick? I'm assuming you've never done any bird, that you belong to that happy section of the community which has never been nobbled. Well, how do you imagine it?

When I ask people – during my spells on the outside, naturally – how they think of life behind bars, I always get the same kind of answer: boring, monotonous, routine. And I would never deny it. There *is* a great deal of boredom, monotony and routine inside. But it is not the whole truth! I would like to emphasise that. It is far from the complete Maud and Ruth! You may have had a day or even a week of boredom, monotony and routine and then – kapow! – you find yourself in the middle of an uproar that would make the Battle of the Somme look like a rest cure.

The Great Pill Hunt started like that. It built up gradually, step by step, without my even perceiving, for a long time, that I was getting involved. Then suddenly Harry Grout was on the doorstep and my life was trembling in the balance. Here's how it went and see if you can spot the stages by which Nemesis – or do I mean Genesis? – some bloke with a big meat-hook – or was it a scythe? – began to tailgate me.

'What are you reading, Fletch?'

I sighed. I have a hospitable nature, very similar to those of the Southern gentlemen I was trying to read about, but I do sometimes crave privacy. Unfortunately, the idea that your home is your castle has never caught on in the nick. Villains and criminals tend, between the hours of lock-up, to treat your home as their own and it is considered doubtful manners to request them to depart. So for the last ten minutes, I had been struggling to keep my attention on my book while acutely conscious that Bunny Warren was seated opposite me.

'What are you reading, Fletch?' he had finally asked.

'A book.'

Irony is, of course, wasted on Bunny but it had the effect of easing my own feelings somewhat. He inquired earnestly : 'No, I meant what sort of book?'

'A paperback sort of book. It consists, Bunny, of lots of bits of paper stuck together down the left-hand side.'

'Is it a good book?'

'I won't know that until I've finished it, will I? And that's going to be a hell of a long time if I get these continual interruptions.'

Warren brooded wistfully and then remarked, 'I'd read books too, if I could read.'

'Still, leaves you more time for deep thinking, don't it?' I said encouragingly.

A faint leer stole across Warren's face, making him look like a dissolute hare, and he asked : 'Here, Fletch, is it a dirty book?'

'Yeah, filthy. I dropped it in the mud on the way back from lunch.'

McLaren arrived then. Just like Warren – not a word of : are you free? Or : could I just have a word with you? Or : sorry to disturb. Not a bit. He just slouched into the old dell and gave it the once over.

'Reading a book, Fletch?' he inquired.

'No, I'm ironing.' But the sooty Scot seemed as impervious to irony as Warren. He actually had the once-a-week to come and read over my shoulder. I said indignantly : 'Would you mind not doing that? Height of bad manners, that is.'

But he just shrugged, sat down and studied the soiled cover of my treasure.

'*Mandingo?* What's that about then?'

'Curiously enough, it's about your lot. Slaves in the deep south.'

'Scottish slaves, are they?'

'Blacks, sonny Jock. Your ancestors. Toiling in the cotton fields.'

'My ancestors are from the West Indies. Half of them are.'

'Same kind of thing. This lot picked cotton. Your lot picked sugar cane or bananas. Comes down to the same thing. A load of blacks toiling in the fields under the hot sun picking things.'

Warren, revealing an unexpected streak of scholarship, remarked, 'I thought slaves were in Roman times. In galleys, rowing like.'

I nodded. 'Well yes, them was your galley slaves.'

Bunny shook his head and groaned. It was obvious he was getting out of his depth. 'But they was white. I know they was because I've seen them in films. Set in Roman times. And they always had slaves in them. And Rosanna Podesta. And Steve Reeves. Did you ever see Jason and the Golden Fleas?'

I laid aside *Mandingo* with a sigh. 'Fleece would be the word you had in mind, Warren, assuming you had a mind.'

'Was Tony Curtis in that one? He's often a Roman.'

'You just don't know your history, Bunny. Tony Curtis hangs about in Ancient Baghdad.'

'What was that other film about Jason? A real smasher that was – oh yes, Jason and the Astronauts.'

McLaren and I exchanged a weary glance. Then McLaren growled: 'You dim nurk, Warren. You mean Jason and the Juggernauts.'

I stood up resolutely. 'If you'll excuse me, Philip Jenkinson, I think this is where I came in. It's the bit where Rod Steiger hits Sidney Poitier over the head with a chamber-pot because he wants to read his book *in peace*!'

This time McLaren, whose intelligence, being about average, towers above Bunny's, got the message. He said apologetically: 'Sorry, Fletch – we're just going.'

'No, get your money's worth. Stay for the final shoot-out. With any luck Jason there might get his argonauts blown off.'

I grabbed up my cup of tea and my book and headed out. As I left, I heard a final intellectual exchange between them.

Warren remarked: 'I didn't think they had guns then.'

'When?'

'Well – like – in the days of Kirk Douglas.'

So there I was, banished from my cell and looking for a quiet spot to have a read. Well, of course, there ain't no quiet spots in the nick so I wound up inevitably in that paradise of rest and recreation, the association area, with its festive benches and tables and dog-eared Monopoly set. There I planted myself next to Lukewarm, one of our dear queens, who was knitting himself a winter bra or something, and again opened my book. But – and this is the point! – fate was already at work. If I hadn't been driven from the dell, I would never have become enmeshed with Grouty and his wayward schemes.

Lukewarm remarked affably: 'Reading a book, Fletch?'

'Oh Gawd, don't you start. Just carry on with your balaclava. There might be another war. In fact, there will be if I don't finish this book.'

But at that point a sound that would have caused a fearless white hunter, accustomed to the hideous noises of the jungle, to freeze in his steps with paling lips, smote our ears. We both looked up at the landing, from whence it had issued. There we beheld that most terrible of predators, the dread MacKay. He was even now closing in on his pathetic prey, little Harris, the slimiest con man of them all. I noticed that Harris still had his arm in a sling as a result of having offended one of the snout barons.

'Stand where you are, Harris!'

'Me, Mr MacKay?'

'Yes, you. Don't move.'

Whereupon the savage creature, eyes glaring and jaws slavering, bore down on the huddled shape.

'Harris, you've been to the medical room.'

'Yes, sir. Just had me plaster changed like.'

'The orderly thinks you may have palmed some pills.'

'Not me, sir.'

'And if you have, by heaven, I'll find them.'

And MacKay naturally started to frisk Harris. I turned to Lukewarm and remarked : 'Never a dull moment.'

Just then a drop of something flew into my eye. I glanced up to see if a half-witted sparrow had come amongst us but all I could discern was MacKay fondling Harris. However, much later in the day I recalled that tiny splash. Enough said?

MacKay, who had had a disappointing grope, snarled : 'Come with me, Harris.'

The one addressed, who had apparently recovered his usual bravado, squealed :

'Listen, I'm clean. You got no right. This is harassment.'

'I'll harass you, Harris, I'm going to strip you down.'

Lukewarm remarked wistfully : 'Some girls have all the luck.' Then he continued : 'He'd whip anything, Harris would. Don't know what he wants with pills.'

'Oh, come on, Lukewarm,' I remonstrated. 'You know

the racket in here. Always someone who wants to be picked up or zonked out. Can't see it meself. Not my cup of tea, drugs.'

This set Lukewarm off. He began recounting an apparently endless tale about his last boy friend's tragic enslavement to some pills known as 'pink whispers'. Still yearning for a read, I picked up my book and tea and stole away back to the flowery, leaving him yarning away to empty space.

'Hello, Fletch,' Lennie greeted me.

I glanced about approvingly. 'They've gone, have they?'

'Who?'

'Warren and McLaren. The Black and White Minstrels.'

'Yes. They've gone to check up on the Thief of Baghdad. They've got a bet about how much he flogged it for.' He went on, 'Hey, I did the lunches on my own today. Did you like it?' Lennie works in the kitchens.

'Yeah. What was the name of that pudding?'

'Tapioca.'

'You couldn't sneak me a dollop back here, could you?'

Lennie beamed. 'You liked it that much, did you?'

'No, but I need something to stick down the sole of me shoe.'

But Lennie was in a cheerful mood. 'I'll ignore that. Tapioca off a chef's back.'

I took a sip of my tea. It was foul. That was only to be expected but by now it was also cold. I shuddered and pushed the cup away.

Lennie asked : 'What was the kerfuffle? I heard MacKay nabbed Harris.'

'Yeah. Thought he'd been pinching pills from the medical officer.'

'Had he?'

'Very likely. But MacKay didn't find anything. Harris must have stashed them.'

'Wish I knew where.'

'Oh? Why? You don't even know what they was.'

'Wouldn't matter to the blokes in here. Could sell them, like.'

'Oh yes? You'd challenge the might and monopoly of genial Harry Grout?'

Lennie shuddered slightly at the thought. 'No, perhaps not. I'd take them myself, then.'

I shook my head sadly. 'Drug addict.'

'Oh, come on, Fletch. Your generation has a lot of prejudices about drugs. It's just fear through ignorance.'

'My generation's sensible enough to know that drugs don't do no one no good no how. They're anathema to me, they are.'

'There's even drugs for that,' Lennie offered.

'What?'

'Anathema.'

'Anathema is an expression, not an ailment.'

'I know. I was only making a joke.'

'Godber,' I said, 'you have used up your joke ration for the month with that tapioca pudding.'

At this point, a hideous scream rent the air. Lennie started. 'What was that?'

'Maybe someone's gone on hunger strike and they're force-feeding him your tapioca.'

'That was a terrible scream, Fletch. Bloodcurdling.'

'Probably one of your drug addict friends taking the cold chicken cure.'

'Cold turkey.'

'Too expensive. They use chicken in here.'

Lennie went to the door and looked out. But he didn't see anything unusual. He returned to his place and remarked: 'You just don't understand, Fletch. Fear through ignorance.'

'Listen, I'm not ignorant. I'm just more aware of the abuses than you seem to be. I've seen it happen. Saw some of my comrades in arms get addicted to morphine.'

'When was this?'

'When I was in the army.'

'Why did they have morphine?'

'To ease the pain of the gunshot wounds.'

'Where was you stationed, a rifle range?'

'You're an impudent nurk, Godber. While you were safely sleeping in your Smethwick crib, some of us was doing our bit for Queen and country. In the steaming Malayan jungle at the height of the terror.'

'You told me you worked in the stores in Kuala Lumpur. There wasn't any fighting there.'

'There was in the stores. Anyway, I'm not talking about that. The point is that two of my best mates got addicted to morphine subsequent to having received gunshot wounds.'

A light of respect dawned in Lennie's eyes. 'Inflicted by the Malayan terrorists?'

'Not exactly. They shot each other in the foot to avoid meeting them.'

Lennie said haughtily : 'Comes as no surprise that that type of person was your best mate.'

'What type of person?'

'Cowards.'

'Oh, it's easy for you to talk. Not being there in the heat and stench. You heard that scream just now. When I was in hospital in Singapore, that would go on all night.'

'It's your own fault. You should have left the nurses alone.'

I reached out to give him a playful clout on the chin and froze. There in the doorway stood the man everyone recognises but no one ever claims a fiver for doing so. It's usually the other way round.

'Oh, hello, Grouty,' I said brightly, hoping my voice didn't quaver.

Lennie sprang to his feet.

'Oh, hello, Mr Grout. Sir.'

Grouty heaved himself into the flowery. 'Hello, Fletch. Goodbye, Godber.'

I could see Lennie hadn't caught on. The kid's a bit dim sometimes and, not wanting to see him provoke Grouty's ire – whatever ire may be – I signalled discreetly at him to naff off. Lennie blinked at me and then caught on.

'Oh – yeah – right,' he stammered. 'I hope you'll excuse me.'

He turned and trotted out of the dell. With a deal more cheerfulness than I felt, I said, 'What's up then, Grouty?'

Grouty seated himself and pressed the tips of his fingers together. 'I just – er – had a word with Harris.'

'Oh yeah?' I asked. Then I recalled the ghastly scream which had rent the air a little while ago. I added: 'I heard you, yes.'

'He whipped some pills.'

'Comes as no surprise.'

'He said that when MacKay frisked him, he dropped them over the landing.'

'Really?'

What Grouty was saying sounded innocent enough but somehow it made me uneasy. On the dashboard of my mind a warning light came on. At Grouty's next remark it flared out like a ruddy beacon.

'Under which there were only two people at the time.'

But I kept my cool and said innocently: 'Yeah, that's right, me and Lukewarm.'

Grouty smiled his special smile which begins just below the eyes. He said gently : 'Well, Lukewarm wouldn't, would he?'

'Wouldn't what, Grouty?'

'Take advantage. Of a windfall.'

Grouty smiled sadly. It made him look fatherly. I once saw him hold that look while Carnera Stubbins, his chief henchman at the time, broke both arms and six ribs of one of his business rivals. He went on :

'I'll explain the problem, Fletch. I want those pills back where they belong.'

'In your pocket?' I suggested.

'Dear me, no. In the M.O.'s office.'

This was a turn-up. I asked warily : 'I didn't know you shared my views on the evils of drugs, Grouty?'

'Not exactly. It's just that despicable pilfering of this nature could mess up my own pill-peddling operation.'

I shook my head. 'I never heard of that one, Grouty.'

'Very few people have. That's one of its virtues. Now, you see the problem? Unless those pills are returned, MacKay is going to ask the M.O. to do an inventory to find out what is missing. Should that happen, they'll find a lot more's missing than they ever imagined.'

I could well believe this. I could also readily grasp the nature of Grouty's problem. What I could not, for the moment, perceive was how I was going to get out of this without acquiring flexible shins.

'Couldn't you replace them from stock?' I suggested.

'I haven't got any stock. I don't keep 'em. I peddle them.'

'Yes, I see your point.'

'Well, we've got an hour.'

'Oh? An hour? We've got an hour, have we?'

'Yes. The doc's over in the married quarters lancing Mrs Barrowclough's boil. That gives us about an hour to replace the pills.'

I tried, without much confidence, a heartfelt appeal. 'Now, Grouty, you and me know each other. I give you my word, which you know is sancro – er sancto – you know it's reliable, Grouty – I give you my word that I ain't got the pills.'

But Grouty contented himself with an understanding nod. 'Not enough time to verify that, Fletch. But what's more to the point is, you're one of the few people in this nick in a position to acquire some more pills.'

'How?'

'Come on, Fletch. You work the admin. block. That means you're in touch with the Governor, secretaries, typists. See, it don't matter what sort of pills they are. Just so long as they're back in the M.O.'s office. Then I'll get the word to MacKay that the matter's been taken care of.'

'Yeah, well that will solve it. But even supposing I can do what you suggest, what sort of pills?'

'Pills is pills, Fletch. Aspirin, allergy pills, slimming pills.'

'Here – those typists are all on the pill. They're all ravers over there.'

'Now steady on, Fletch, there are limits. If you whip those and the M.O. issues them to some poor bloke with toothache, what then?'

'Stop his teeth getting pregnant, won't it?' I suggested, but Grouty didn't smile. 'Oh, I see. It's a serious matter, isn't it. Well, I can't guarantee anything, Grouty, but I'll do the best I can.'

He nodded and his nose smiled again. 'I'm sure you will, Fletch.' He turned to go and then turned back. This time his eyes joined in the fun. 'Oh, if you see any codeine, get some for Harris. It seems his arm has been playing him up.' Chuckling softly, he ambled out of one Englishman's besieged castle.

A few minutes later, Lennie returned.

'What were that all about?'

'Grouty wants me to whip some pills for him.'

'Why?'

'To replace the ones Harris whipped.'

'Well, where are the pills Harris whipped?'

'Precisely,' I said bitterly. 'Where are the peppers that Peter Piper picked? If we knew that, sonny Jim, there'd be no problem, would there? Listen, you know the druggies in here. They're your precious generation. Who's likely to have any pills?'

Lennie looked thoughtful. 'The biggest freaks are those three in the end cell in B Block. One's on pills. One's on grass. And one's on booze. We call them pillhead, pothead and –'

'I can work it out. Listen, you're off duty. Can you get to them?'

'Bit tricky. Them three work in the postage room.'

'Which doubtless explains why our mail deliveries are so erratic.'

'Barrowclough has lots of pills.'

'He has?'

'All sorts. Nerve pills, indigestion pills, and he's also a vitamin freak. I should think when he makes love he rattles.'

'Well, he won't be doing much rattling at present. His old lady has a boil in a very nasty place.'

'Where?' Lennie asked eagerly.

'The screws' married quarters. What's more the M.O. is with her at this moment with his pike or lance or whatever. That's why we've got about fifty minutes to find them pills.'

'We?'

'Oh, come on, Godber. You're supposed to be my mate, aren't you?'

54

'I am your mate, Fletch. Always have been and always will be, I hope.'

'Then help me get some flipping pills.'

'I'd like to, Fletch, but for one thing.'

'What's that?'

The young nurk grinned. 'You told me not to have anything to do with drugs.'

I involuntarily raised my arm to give him a swift clip on the ear and just then Barrowclough waddled in. I froze. Barrowclough exclaimed : 'Fletcher !'

'What?'

'Do I see a raised arm?'

'I've no idea. Oh, you mean this arm? No, this arm is not a raised arm, Mr Barrowclough. This is a flexed arm. It's set rigid. Muscular stress. A nervous condition. I wish I had something for nerves. A pill or something.'

'I have pills for my nerves.'

'What an incredible coincidence.' I lowered my arm with much difficulty. 'Are you telling me, Mr Barrowclough, you have something which can alleviate my suffering?'

'Well, I don't carry them around with me.'

'You don't? No, I noticed you weren't rattling.'

'They're on prescription, you see. They're only mild tranquillisers, but they help me cope with the horrors of life.'

'Really? How is Mrs Barrowclough?'

'Not too good, I'm afraid. As you know, she's not the easiest of women to live with at the best of times but now that she can't sit down.'

'So that's where it is.'

'What?'

'The boil.'

Barrowclough blinked in surprise. 'How did you know about my wife's boil?'

'Oh, it just leaked out.'

'We're hoping a hot poultice will help.'

'You want to slap a dollop of Godber's tapioca pudding on it. Of course, a lot of these complaints are caused by lack of vitamins. You don't have any vitamin pills do you, Mr Barrowclough?'

'Every morning I take vitamin A, vitamin B, high protein and three hundred milligrams of vitamin C. I've always been a great believer in vitamins. I think that's why I have such a good complexion.'

'That's very interesting. I suspect my nerves are caused by vitamin deficiency. You haven't any to spare, have you, Mr Barrowclough?'

'Oh, I think I have, yes. I'll bring you some in the morning.'

'Be too late then.'

'Well, your nerves aren't going to crumble overnight.'

'I was thinking more of my kneecaps.'

'I don't think I follow.'

'I shan't be able to either with broken kneecaps. No seriously, Mr Barrowclough, the main problem with my nerves and lack of vitamins is the terrible indigestion it brings on. Specially Lennie's tapioca.'

'I do me best with the ingredients I get,' Godber intruded indignantly. 'The chef said my raspberry blancmange was the finest he'd ever tasted.'

I ignored this boast. 'You don't happen to have anything for indigestion, do you, Mr Barrowclough?'

'I certainly do. Where's your mug?'

And the nurk produced from his pocket two giant alka-seltzer tablets, wrapped in foil. I shook my head. 'No use for them. They're too big.'

'Too big?'

'I mean – my digestion's so weak I can't even digest alka-seltzer.'

Barrowclough frowned maternally. He looked like a cow whose calf is running a slight fever. 'I must say you seem in pretty poor shape, Fletcher.'

'I can stand most of it. If it wasn't for the blinding headaches.'

'Fletcher, I think you'd better report on sick parade tomorrow. Get a couple of codeine from the M.O. And now I must get on.'

And he departed.

I sighed deeply. 'That was no flaming help.' Then I turned on Lennie. 'And nor was you.'

'Not talking to you,' he said sulkily.

'What?'

'Not talking to you.'

'Just proved yourself wrong. Why not?'

'Had enough of your derogatory remarks about my culinary prowess.'

'Your culinary prowess is of no consequence compared to the urgent matter at hand. Do you realise I have less than an hour to find some replacement pills.'

'Better get to work then, hadn't you?'

I uttered a bitter laugh. 'I'll not forget this, Godber.'

Lennie shrugged. 'If you can't get any, you can't. Grouty's problem, not yours.'

'Oh right. I hadn't thought of that. And I'm sure Grouty will also take on the problem of finding me a wheelchair. Listen, son, when genial Harry Grout asks a favour, it is with the clear understanding that the favour will be done. If it isn't, he takes it as a personal affront. He sends Crusher Watson round to curtail your mobility.'

'That'll solve your problem then – you'll end up in hospital. No shortage of pills there.'

I was shaking my head, more in sorrow than anger, when Harris slithered into the dell.

'Hello, Fletch.'

'You've got a bleeding nerve, Harris.'

'What?'

'Showing your face round here.'

'Why not?'

'Because you're the cause of all the bleeding trouble.'

'Okay, I took them. But I haven't got them now.'

'What do you want then?'

'I heard of your problem, Fletch. I know that Grouty has given you the favour of getting him some more pills.'

'I don't deny it.'

'I could maybe help you there.'

'How?'

'I know where I could lay me hands on some.'

'Well, why didn't you tell Grouty that in the first place?'

'It's delicate, see. Fact is, today wasn't the first time I nicked pills. But I never knew about Grouty's racket. Well, if he knew I'd taken some before – ' Harris hugged his plastered arm protectively.

'What sort of pills have you been snatching?' Lennie asked.

'All kinds. Always a market in here, isn't there? Uppers, downers, twisters, benders.'

'Let me get this straight, Harris,' I said. 'What you're saying is you've still got the proceeds of previous thefts intact?'

'Could be.'

'Which you will give to me and I will hand on to Grouty, pretending I got them elsewhere?'

'That's right. I think it's a very noble gesture on my part. Get us both out of the clarts, right?'

'Very noble, Harris. Let's have them then.'

'Hold your horses.'

'What?'

Harris smiled like a coy maiden. 'Depends, doesn't it?'

'Depends on what?'

'How much?'

At this dastardly remark, I felt the blood drumming in my temples. I repeated : 'How much !'

'Fair do's. I'll give you a fair price, Fletch.'

'Harris, you are – words fail me.'

Lennie said earnestly : 'Has it ever occurred to you, Harris, that there's more to life than turning a quick quid? There's things like comradeship, honour and decency?'

Harris looked dubious. 'Is there?'

I silenced Lennie with a lofty wave.

'Don't appeal to his better nature, son, because he ain't got none. There's only one language that the Harrises of this world understand and that's the language I intend to use in future negotiations.'

Harris shot me a suspicious look. 'What's that, Fletch?'

My reply was to move towards him. He began to back away. Lennie suddenly felt an urgent call of nature and hurried out of the flowery, closing the door behind him. A moment later, the long-delayed echo of the terrible scream we had heard earlier rang round the nick.

'Come in, Fletch,' called Grouty, some time later when I knocked at his palatial door. I entered, marvelling as always at the level of luxury he enjoyed in prison. Carpets, curtains, pictures, lamps, radio – the interior would not have disgraced a charming bungalow in Walthamstow. 'What kept you?'

He grinned at me and I grinned back.

'Well, you said it was a matter of urgency, Grouty. Just for the record, these aren't the original pills, which I have never seen. I had to get these ones using all my ingenuity.'

'Yes, I heard you using it, Fletch.'

'I just hope that this puts me at the bottom of your "favours to be done by" list.'

'No question, Fletch.'

'What a lunch hour. I never even finished my cup of tea. And now I've got to get back to work.'

'No peace for the wicked,' he said, lying down on his bed.

'Don't you have work to go to, Grouty?'

'I'm on light duties, Fletch. They put me in charge of the swimming pool.'

'But we ain't got one.'

Grouty nodded. 'I know.'

'Oh – clerical error, was it?'

'Something like that. That's why time hangs so heavy on my hands.'

'Oh dear me. Well, I'd best be off then. Don't want to interrupt your boredom.' I was backing deferentially towards the door when I saw them: lovely, glowing, coloured things. My mouth watered. 'Aren't those crystallised fruits, Grouty?'

He glanced indifferently at the treasure.

'Yes.'

'My favourite them.'

'Really?' asked Grouty. 'Mine too.'

The delicious edibles slipped from his thoughts. He opened the packet of pills I had brought him. 'Any idea what these are, Fletch?'

'Does it matter? You said yourself : a pill is a pill.'

'Still, you got to be careful with drugs. These could be dangerous.'

'Well, yes, best be on the safe side. Try 'em out in the Governor's tea. See you.'

And with a last wishful look at the tempting sweetmeats, I turned on my heel and departed.

When I got back to the dell, I was displeased to find

Lennie reading my paperback. Not only that but he had ensconced himself in my cosy top bunk to do so.

'What are you doing in my bunk, Godber?' I asked the impudent young nurk.

'More light up here.'

'To read *my* book by. Give it here.'

And I grabbed the volume from his grasp. He sighed and swung himself off the bunk. 'I only borrowed it.'

'Lost my place, didn't you?'

Lennie said dreamily, 'That's a good scene, Fletch, where the plantation owner gets hold of the nubile young slave girl behind the cotton gin and – '

I interrupted him indignantly. 'Just shut up, will you? Blimey, I hadn't even reached that scene. You've had a hard afternoon, haven't you?'

'I'm entitled to my rest. Up at four, me. It's no joke, you know, frying five hundred eggs at dawn.'

'You want to make one vast omelette and let them get on with it.'

I glanced about at the untidy state of the homestead. 'You could have tidied up a bit. I mean, look at this place. You haven't even washed the mugs out.'

I took them over to the sink and emptied the slops. Out of mine fell a small packet. I took it up in surprise.

'Here – what's this?'

'What's what?' asked Lennie.

'Look.' I showed him.

'Where's that come from?'

'It was in the tea.'

'Well, open it.'

I did so and emptied into my hand eight small white pills. I frowned. 'What are they?'

Lennie peered at the hoard. 'Can't be sure. Could be amphetamine. Or maybe Bennies.'

'Whose?'

'Benzedrine. How did they get in your tea?'

But I was no longer listening. I'd got it. The splash! The little splash in my eye in Funland earlier. It must have been the pills, dumped skilfully by Harris, falling into my teacup. A pulse of fury went through me. A lunch-hour of terror and intimidation and I'd had the flaming goods in my hand all the time! I exclaimed:

'These must have been Harris's. And they fell into me tea from above.'

Lennie grinned. 'Bennies from heaven.'

'Oh, belt up, Godber.'

He shook his head. 'When you think of all the trouble you went to and they was under your nose all the time.'

'So – the whole thing was a storm in a teacup.'

Just then an animal bark, readily recognisable as the voice of Mr MacKay, sounded from the landing outside.

'Move, you men! Don't lounge around on the landing!'

The voice was approaching rapidly. And I was holding a handful of terrible contrabrand. Lennie jumped up and pointed at the pills. 'Quick! Get rid of them!'

I gazed about desperately. 'Yeah, but where? If he's doing a search?'

'We'll have to swallow them.'

Just in time I slipped Lennie half and then we swallowed four each. MacKay appeared in the door before they'd even gone down.

'What's wrong with you two? You look like you've swallowed a frog.'

I gulped which helped the pills down some.

'Nothing, Mr MacKay.'

But his head swivelled like a periscope as he inspected us.

'I know when men are acting suspicious. Anything to hide, Fletcher?'

'No, sir.'

'Godber?'

'No, sir.'

There was a faint sound from floor level. I groaned inwardly. The pill container had slipped off the table. MacKay swung round like a gun-dog, only not as lovable. He pointed.

'What's that? What's that?'

'What's what, Mr MacKay?'

'Pick it up, Godber,' ordered Slade's own Führer.

Lennie did so and handed it silently to MacKay. He examined it gingerly as if afraid it might go off.

'Well? What is it?'

'Just a – a thing, sir,' I murmured feebly, wondering if the singing in my ears was a sign that the end was nigh.

'A thing that looks like a container for pills.'

Lennie contributed. 'That's right, sir. Just a couple for Fletcher's indigestion.'

I confirmed. 'I get this terrible indigestion on account of the vitamin deficiency affecting me nerve endings.'

MacKay squinted suspiciously.

'Pills are a dirty word in this prison. I nearly caught Harris with some this morning.'

'What can you expect, sir, from a nurk like Harris?'

MacKay chuckled, the way he does when a new punishment occurs to him. He remarked: 'Well, the doctor told me what they were. I can't help hoping Harris swallowed the lot.'

Lennie and I managed to exchange a glance which was not exactly brimful of cheer.

'What would happen to him, sir, if he did?' I asked.

'Hard to say for sure. They were the doctor's own pills, for worming his spaniel. All right, carry on.'

He spun round on his heel like a drill sergeant gone berserk and marched out.

I tottered to the bunks and lowered myself carefully.

In a small, hollow voice, Lennie asked: 'How do you feel, Fletch?'

'Rowf!' I replied. 'Rowf! Rowf! Rowf!'

Poetic Justice

The nick makes strange bed-fellows. Well, in fact, sharing a bed is frowned on by the authorities and I did not mean to imply anything dodgy. What I meant was that it's amazing who turns up. I know that some noble poet suggested it would be smashing if the lion was to lie down with the lamb. But does it happen? How many lions have you seen kipping with lambs? The only place it would be at all likely to occur would be in one of Her Majesty's correctional establishments if they was both doing bird. Then they would have no choice but to flock together. And that is exactly what happened when Rawley moved in with us. But, you might reasonably be expected to ask, which was the lion and which the lamb? Naturally, I have my own views but, after hearing the facts, you can decide for yourself.

It started one fine day when, apart from being an outcast felon with years of incarceration ahead of me, I hadn't a care in the world. I was strolling along the landing, singing at the top of my voice :

'Some enchanted evening,
    You may see a stranger – '

I was not distressed by the abusive cries which issued from the cells I passed. I had just won an ounce of snout from a trustee called Turnbull and such small triumphs in the nick lift the heart like a big score on the stock exchange to your free hustler. Since I was so chuffed the blow, when it fell, was terrible indeed. Now I don't mean that some philistine stepped out of his cell and donged me with a slop bucket. Nothing so crude. Still

65

c

singing, I turned into the happy home and – the song withered on my lips.

The first thing I saw was Harris's face. This was quite bad enough since it is a spectacle which has been known to cause new arrivals, doing their first spell of porridge, to cringe whimpering against the wall. But the next thing I saw was even worse. It was a bed. What, you ask, nothing so terrible about that? Do beds have sharp teeth and knobbly fists? Maybe not. But they have something worse. They have occupants. True, this particular bed was as yet unoccupied but that was, in the circumstances, far from reassuring. Am I making myself clear? In addition to the two familiar bunks in the old flowery, which are the havens of myself and my cell-mate, Lennie, there was now an additional bed. That could only mean one thing. They were putting a third into the dell. Of course, we had had rumours for weeks that, because of general overcrowding, such a calamity was on the cards. But somehow I had never thought it would strike me. The third thing I saw in my ruined home was the bovine face of Mr Barrowclough, quivering nervously in anticipation of my reaction, and the fourth thing was Lennie. I said in a steely voice.

'What have we here?'

Barrowclough bolted for the door.

'I'm just off, Fletcher.'

'Oh no,' I said, barring the way, 'you're not.'

'But, Fletcher – '

I pointed distastefully. 'What is that object?'

'What object?'

'That bed. What is it?'

'Well, it's – a bed.'

'And just why is that bed in my already overcrowded cell? Even more to the point, why is horrible Harris here? There'd better not be a connection between them.'

Harris squealed indignantly, ' 'Ere, I only brung it here.'

I turned on him. 'Good, then you can brung it out again.'

Barrowclough cleared his throat and mooed. 'Fletcher, an alarming rise in crime rates in this country has caused an extra burden on an already overworked penal system.'

'Oh yes?'

'This in turn has meant that prisons have had to stretch their already limited resources to try and accommodate the extra influx of convicted felons, which they're ill-equipped to deal with in the first place.'

I played it very cool. Nodding sympathetically, I murmured : 'Very interesting. Highly illuminating.'

Barrowclough breathed a sigh of relief. 'Well, as long as you appreciate our difficult position.'

I nodded sagely. 'I do, yes. We've all got to make the best of this difficult situation. Now shift that bed out of here.'

Barrowclough drew himself up as if rejecting the advances of some persistent bull. 'Fletcher, a new arrival is moving in here and that's that.'

'It's just not on, Mr Barrowclough. I mean, look at this place. It was designed by the same architect what done the Black Hole of Calcutta.'

'Fletcher, neither of us have any choice in the matter, so you may as well accept it as a fait accompli.'

And, since I'd carelessly shifted a few steps away from the door, he managed to slip out.

Harris glanced at me dubiously. That toad has tasted my displeasure on more than one occasion and he sensed that I was in an ugly mood. He edged towards the door. 'I'll be off then, Fletch. Bit crowded in here. I hope the three of you will be very happy.'

'Naff off, Harris,' I grunted.

As he obeyed, he courted disaster by snarling: 'Naff off yourself, Fletch. With knobs on.'

But I was too downhearted even to aim a kick at his fleeing backside. I sat down and began rolling myself a snout. Lennie remarked: 'I'm afraid the whole rhythm of our lives is in some jeopardy, Fletch.'

'Flaming outrage. What's the word, then?'

'Well, I had a word with Davey Greener who works in reception. He says there's three come in today. One of them's a bit of a mystery. Name's Rawley. He was never documented.'

This was strange. 'How do you mean?'

'The screws just whipped him off some place. No documentation, no mug shots.'

'Really?'

'Me and the lads were speculating. Reckoned he was maybe a hard case. You know, from a firm or something.'

'Not in this nick. They don't have heavies up here. Except for Harry Grout. And he won't stand no competition.'

'I think they whipped him straight up to the Governor.'

'Maybe he's a celebrity. Maybe a rock star on a drug bust and they took him off for a press conference.'

'He was no rock star. Kind of bald and plump with flat feet.'

'Might be Elton John.'

'No, he walked like a pregnant duck.'

'You should know better than that, Godber.'

'Better than what?'

'That. Drawing attention to people's physical peculiarities. I've noticed you doing it a lot recently. I was saying to Taffy, young people today are always taking the mick out of folks because they're too tall or too fat or walk with bow legs or something.'

'Who's Taffy?'

'You know him – bloke in the hobby shop. Fat guy with ears like jug handles.' And I lit my snout.

Meanwhile, back in the old Governor's office – ah but, you are asking yourself, how do I know what was transpiring in the Governor's office? I know because one of the two embarrassed middle-aged men facing each other across his desk was soon to occupy the third bed in my dell and he told me all about it later.

As soon as the orderly had withdrawn, leaving them alone, the Governor did something very surprising. He hurried round from behind his desk and, stretching out his hand, said warmly : 'Steven !'

The newly-arrived convict took his hand and shook it without enthusiasm. He said : 'Hello, Geoffrey.'

'I thought we should have a little chat before we document you. But – what can I say?'

'Perhaps the less said, the better.'

Then Mr Venables, the Governor of Slade Prison, actually got a chair and seated his new inmate. As he did so, he remarked, 'Tragic ! How's Marjorie taking all this?'

'As well as can be expected. And how are you, Geoffrey?'

'Oh, I'm all right.'

'And Muriel?'

'Busy as ever. She has her committees. I have my prison.'

'Haven't seen you both for such a long time.'

The Governor exclaimed impulsively : 'You must come round to dinner.' Then he frowned and shook his head sadly. 'Oh no, of course, you won't be able to. Silly me.'

Rawley, his unlikely guest, said : 'Not unless my appeal comes through, no.'

'This whole thing is most embarrassing for me.'

Rawley smiled wryly. 'It's a little worse than that for me. The entire fabric of my life has collapsed.'

'I know, but see it from my point of view. We were at Winchester together. In the Guards together. We're members of the same club.'

'We won't be for much longer. They've asked for my resignation.'

'Still, our relationship is going to create a bit of a problem.'

'Is there any reason why people should become aware of it?'

'Perhaps not. There isn't anyone from the old school here, thank God.'

'There's everything else though – officers, clubmen, Rotarians. In the shower, an embezzler came up to me and gave me a Masonic handshake.'

'There you are.'

'I don't want to plead special treatment, of course, but couldn't you separate me in a single cell, with a few books?'

'Fatal. Can't have secrets in here. It would cause speculation. And resentment. Best thing is to slip you into a cell with other men.'

'But I'd be with a bunch of common criminals.'

Mr Venables coughed discreetly. 'With due respect, Steven, since the verdict you *are* a common criminal.'

Rawley said excitedly, 'Surely you can do something. We went through the war together.'

'Only the last three months.'

'Have you forgotten that I saved your life?'

Venables considered this for a moment and then admitted : 'Yes.'

'What, you've forgotten Paris? Armistice night? The George the Fifth hotel? We were both pie-eyed and I stopped you falling down a lift shaft.'

Venables shook his head sadly. 'I don't drink, Steven. Never have.'

Rawley blinked and then sighed. 'I felt sure it was you. Must have been Thunderbox Wallis.'

At this point, the touching reunion was interrupted by a knock at the door, and in marched Mr MacKay. He shot Rawley a contemptuous look and then addressed Venables.

'You sent for me, sir?'

'Ah yes, Mr MacKay – close the door, please. Good. Now, I wanted to discuss a delicate situation with you. This is an old friend of mine, Mr Rawley, who will be with us for a while.'

MacKay, true to his nature, immediately fawned on the bald little man. 'Pleased to meet you, sir. Will you be staying for lunch?'

Rawley smiled faintly. 'If my appeal fails, I'll be staying for three years.'

Some time later, I was sitting in the day room, basking in *The Sun*. With me were Lennie, Bunny Warren and the sooty Glaswegian, McLaren. Before long, the peace and good-fellowship were broken by a reptilian sound.

'Ere, listen,' hissed Harris, '' 'ave you met your new room-mate yet?'

I sighed and kept my eyes fixed to the female form divine. 'Still have that pleasure to come.'

'Hope it isn't Turner,' Lennie remarked.

'Who?' I asked.

'Turner. One of the new arrivals. He's been on remand since Christmas. Sounds a nasty bit of work. Know what he done?'

'What?' Bunny asked.

'He mugged the Santa Claus at Selfridges.'

I shook my head in sorrow. 'What a charmless offence.'

Lennie grinned. 'He paid for it, though. What he

didn't know was that Santa Claus was an out-of-work wrestler known as Abdul the Turk.'

McLaren whistled. 'What happened?'

'Abdul gave him the aeroplane spin. Spun him from soft toys to electrical appliances.'

'Took on a wrestler once myself,' I remarked.

There were sceptical murmurs. I silenced them by saying firmly, 'Truth. I was in a transport caff on the M6. And I got into an argument with this wrestler over whose sixpence was in the jukebox. The discussion became quite heated and in the end we had a real barney.'

Lennie said: 'Straight – you took on a wrestler, Fletch?'

I nodded, the light of reminiscence shining in my eyes. 'It was a tremendous contest – but she beat me in the end.'

They all stared at me blankly. I know that wit is like the Concorde to most cons, about ten miles over their heads, but I had hoped that Lennie – then I saw the lad was gazing past me intently. He exclaimed: 'Here, that's him – the mystery man. Him with MacKay.'

Naturally I turned, and we all had a butcher's at the balding little man now approaching beside Good Deed MacKay. But at the first glance, a shiver of recognition ran down my spine. Not only of recognition but of incredulity as well. It couldn't be and yet – the distant memory formed in my mind. Three years ago – the court-room – Middlesex Assizes – it *was* him! Not the slightest doubt. MacKay barked.

'All right, you men. This is Rawley, who's moving in with Fletcher and Godber. I don't know what you have heard about him but I want you to treat him just like any other prisoner – understood?'

And having thus established that Rawley was different from other prisoners and quite certain to be treated differently, MacKay spun round on his heel and shunted off. Rawley hesitated and glanced at us diffidently. He said timidly, 'Good afternoon.'

Lennie said cheerfully, 'Afternoon. My name's Godber. You're in with us.'

Rawley nodded and attempted a little smile. I could stand it no longer. I rose to my feet and exclaimed, 'God preserve us!'

Rawley drew back a little and said, 'I'm sorry?'

Lennie, seeing that something was up, said quickly, 'Oh, this is Fletch. He's with us and all.'

'Really?' said Rawley.

I shook my head and said loudly, 'You don't remember me, do you?'

Rawley looked at me doubtfully. 'Your face is vaguely familiar, but I can't quite – '

'Middlesex Assizes? Three years ago?'

'Did you two do a job together or something?' Warren asked interestedly.

'Do a job?' I exclaimed. 'No, we didn't do a job together. He's only the judge who bleeding sent me here!'

This naturally produced not a few murmurs from the assembled felons. They gaped at Judge Rawley as a convention of vegetarians might have done if a pork butcher had intruded on them. I continued, with not a little sarcasm, 'The Honourable Judge Steven Rawley! In all his majesty. How the mighty are fallen.'

Rawley blinked unhappily. 'I'm sorry, but I still don't quite recollect – '

'Why should you? I am merely one of a thousand faces who come before you, while you weigh our lives in the balance of what you call justice!'

Rawley's perplexed expression cleared as if by magic. 'It's Fletcher, isn't it?'

'Oh, you remember now?'

He nodded vigorously. 'I remember your rhetoric. I remember your endless protestations of innocence.'

'Which you were deaf to,' I exclaimed bitterly.

'But you *were* guilty, Fletch,' Lennie said diplomatically. 'You've told us that.'

I turned on him haughtily. 'That is beside the point, Godber.'

'It did seem relevant when I passed sentence,' Rawley offered diffidently.

I addressed my fellow sufferers. 'The point is that this man was not fit to sentence me, as his presence here indicates.'

Warren said uncertainly, 'But he's still a judge. Least, he were at the time.'

'Yeah, but obviously a bent one,' McLaren countered. 'When you're sent down it's one thing knowing it's by an upright pillar of society. But Fletcher's been sent down by a fellow con.'

I nodded agreement with these sentiments.

'Thank you, Jock. This man is no different from me. How do you think I feel being sent down by a crook like me?'

'A judge inside. That's worse than mugging Santa Claus,' Lennie murmured wonderingly.

McLaren asked Rawley, a trifle belligerently. 'What did they bust you for, then?'

'Excuse me?'

'What were the charges against you?'

Rawley immediately intoned, like a Clerk of Court: 'I was indicted on three counts for corruption at common law. These were : accepting an illicit payment as an officer of the Crown; party to a criminal conspiracy; and tampering with evidence with intent to falsify, alter or destroy – '

I cut him off contemptuously.

'Yes, yes, we all know. Plain bribery and corruption. Don't camouflage it behind all that legal mumbo jumbo, Judge Rawley.'

'I have no wish to camouflage anything. As I instructed my counsel : "Let light be shed on this whole sorry affair. Let's bring it out into the open. Let there be no half-truths or evasions." '

'Well, that's refreshingly honest,' Lennie said appreciatively. 'So you're admitting you're guilty then?'

Rawley said loftily : 'I refuse to discuss the matter, pending my appeal.'

'You're bound to get off,' McLaren growled. 'Old school tie, top lawyers.'

Rawley sighed. 'If the lawyers were that good, I'd be out on bail now.'

I sniffed contemptuously. 'Listen, it's a token stretch. Most of what you call us common folk never get the chance of bail. Some blokes are inside for months pending appeal.'

'The same law sent him down what sent us down, Fletcher,' Lennie said firmly.

'What are you saying, Godber?'

'I think his presence here is very reassuring. It's a vindication of our legal system. It proves that no one is beyond the reach of the law.'

'Well, I just ask myself, for everyone of his kind they nobble how many's getting away with it? The bloke who sent him up is probably worse than he is.'

Rawley surprised us then by bursting out in an agonised voice : 'Don't you think I have a conscience? Can you imagine what it's been like, to live a lie?'

I put a stop to this sob stuff by saying firmly, 'Course we can. We're criminals. We does it all the time.'

At this point, looking like a fugitive from the stockyards, Mr Barrowclough ambled in.

'How are you lads improving the sunshine hour?'

'We was just getting aquainted with our distinguished friend,' I advised him.

Mr Barrowclough eyed us narrowly. 'Oh, you know who he is then?'

'We met professionally, so to speak.'

'I see. Well, you must treat Rawley no differently from any other prisoner.'

McLaren muttered darkly, which in a sense he can't help : 'We will if you will.'

'What's that supposed to mean, McLaren?'

'Don't show no favours.'

'Rawley will get no favours from me.' The soft-hearted but determined screw addressed the erstwhile judge. 'Whatever you were before, you're just a number now. A statistic. A set of fingerprints. You're a mug shot, like the rest of these men. You'll pay your dues to society the same way they do. Is that understood?'

Rawley nodded. 'Yes.'

Barrowclough frowned. 'Yes, what?'

'Yes, Mr Barrowclough,' Lennie whispered.

Rawley quickly amended, 'Yes, Mr Barrowclough.'

The screw nodded in satisfaction. 'That's better. Now we must see about getting you a job. Could you come this way, please, your honour?'

That night, I returned to the flowery after taking a shower and found Godber making up Rawley's bed. I stopped aghast. In fact, after Barrowclough's kow-towing earlier, I felt I'd stopped two or three ghasts. I said severely :

'Just what are you doing, Godber?'

'Oh, just making his bed up. He couldn't do it himself.'

'Well, I suggest you encourage him to bleeding learn. Either that or get yourself a little frilly apron.'

'Oh, come on, Fletch, go easy on him. He's lonely. He's afraid. Just like I was, me first night.'

'He's the enemy within. Within my cell, what's more!'

'No he ain't, Fletch. He *was* a judge but now he's a con like the rest of us.'

This innocence disgusted me. 'Don't you believe it. He's the establishment, he is. And I don't fancy the establishment breathing down my neck all day and all night. You must admit it's a bit unusual, Godber.'

'What is?'

'Well, when a judge sentences you to five years, you don't expect him to come in with you.'

At this moment, the fallen magistrate entered. 'Oh, you've made my bed up, Godber? That's most kind.'

'Ovaltine or Horlicks, your honour?' I asked solicitously.

'Excuse me?'

'And what colour do you want your brown shoes polished?'

'Leave off, Fletch,' Lennie urged.

But my justifiable resentment at having to kip with my natural enemy would not permit it. I said sarcastically: 'I suppose you've just been having a nightcap with the Governor?'

Rawley shook his head resentfully. 'Look, I have no influence with the Governor. If I had, I'd be in a single cell with a few books instead of sharing a cell with people like – '

His voice trailed off in confusion, as they say. I concluded the line for him.

'People like us – go on, say it! Listen, let me tell you something about people like us. We don't make no alibis. We deserve to be here. But compared to you, there's something very honest about our dishonesty. Because the worst sort of crime hides behind a mask of respectability.

Some people – people like us – have no way of getting things except to take them. People like you had it all, but it wasn't enough. You wanted more.'

He hung his head.

'I have no defence. Everything you say is completely true. I've been a fool and a hypocrite. But it's not been easy to live with. If you knew the sleepless nights I've spent.'

'Oh yes, I can picture you, tossing and turning on that king-sized Slumberland in that palatial mansion. Personally, I could put up with a little insomnia, if I had a croquet lawn and a tennis court and a Rolls-Royce. That would cushion the pain of a guilty conscience, wouldn't it, Lennie?'

But Rawley protested : 'I don't drive a Rolls-Royce. I've made do with the same Mercedes for three years now.'

'Oh, you poor deprived nurk.'

Lennie surprised me by saying heatedly, 'Pack it in, Fletch. He's a criminal now. Are you saying only the poor and underprivileged like us have any right to be one? Don't the rich have a right to be criminals as well?'

'They better not try. The unions would be on to them straightaway.'

'Oh, don't be stupid.'

'You're being stupid, Godber, and also naïve.'

'I'm just annoyed because you're so inconsistent, Fletch.'

'I'm what?'

'Inconsistent in your attitude. Inside is not out there. Inside's another world. And once inside, anybody has the right to prove himself an OK bloke. *You* told me that. That's why we should never ask what a bloke's in for. So we don't prejudice their chance of making it in here. We're all equal. We only have one enemy, that's the screws. And we only have one purpose in life, that's screwing the system.'

Well, naturally I was pleased that my tuition had been so effective but I felt the lad could have chosen a better moment to demonstrate it.

'Very eloquent all of a sudden, aren't you, son?'

'He's one of us now. That's all I'm saying.'

Rawley plucked up his courage to say : 'The boy is right. I know we've always been on opposite sides of the fence. You're the sort of people I'd normally cross the street to avoid. But the fence is down now.'

I sighed and shook my head. 'I still think the gulf between us is immeasurably wide. I mean, Lennie and me, and most of the lads in here, we come from the same background, ran the same streets. They're a little different from your streets. Your streets have rich kids riding round on bicycles waving tennis rackets. Rows of elm trees and hand-carved privet hedges. Don't have no problems on your streets.'

'Yes, we do. I had to spend fifteen hundred pounds last year on Dutch elm disease.'

'Yeah, and I bet you took your elms to Harley Street, didn't you?'

Rawley said humbly, 'Look, I know you're bound to feel cynical. I understand your attitude, but we all have one thing in common – we're in trouble.'

Lennie supported him. 'He's right, Fletch.'

'Okay, I'm just clearing the air, just letting you know my feelings.'

'I promise I shall be as unobtrusive as possible,' Rawley announced.

I looked at his bed which was about as unobtrusive as a helicopter on a tennis court.

'Well, get yourself a hammock then.'

As I started to undress for another prison night, Lennie

tried to reassure Rawley. 'He's a miserable old git. Listen, these are the rules of the house. Top bunk's his. Seniority like. No one reads the paper till he's through with it. It's best to speak only when spoken to, and his is the toothpaste with the marked tube.'

'I have my own toilet requisites,' Rawley said.

'Just as well,' I grunted.

'Never borrow anything of Fletcher's without express permission,' Lennie urged.

I felt that criticism was implied. 'I am not mean, Godber, if that's what you're hinting. It's just that I don't believe in giving anybody anything. What one has one keeps.'

'Oh, come on, Fletch,' Lennie protested. 'You *are* mean.'

'No, I'm not. Thrifty perhaps. Frugal. Necessary survival technique in here.'

Lennie, unnecessarily I felt, informed Rawley, 'He unwraps Bounty Bars under water so I can't hear he's got one.'

Rawley said smugly : 'I'll be only too willing to share any of the few things they've allowed me to keep.'

This was too good an opportunity. 'Like I said, bribery and corruption. He's at it again.'

'I only meant –'

'Just get yourself to bed, will you, Judge Jeffreys.'

Rawley made a last attempt at conciliation. 'Well, let me say that whatever rules you make, I will go along with them.'

As I hoisted myself up to my bunk, I heard Lennie explain : 'Oh, we're very democratic in here. Fletcher decides and we agree.'

The screw on night duty slammed the cell door.

I turned to the *Sun*. There was a fascinating story in it about a dog that some villain had trained to nick handbags. They'd caught the dog but not the owner and the police were thinking of bringing the animal to trial. It seemed this was still possible according to some ancient law. How do you plead? Wowf, wowf! As I marvelled, I listened at the same time to the conversation between Lennie and Rawley.

'Want some snout?' Lennie asked.

'Excuse me?'

'Should I roll you one?'

'One what?'

'A cigarette.'

'Oh, I don't, thank you. Only very occasionally.'

'It's currency in here, snout.'

'Really?' He sighed.

'You don't look too chipper.'

'Since the door slammed shut, I've realised what prison is about.'

'I know the feeling. This is my first stretch, you know. But stir's a state of mind and survival's in your own head. His highness up there taught me that. The first year is the worst and – sorry, I shouldn't joke.'

'No, please, you shouldn't feel sorry for me.'

'Oh, but I do. I mean, you had a lot more to lose than the rest of us : position, respect. It's the classic story of a man who had it all and blew it all in a moment of weakness.'

I'd finished the dog story and was now intent on their conversation. I intruded sarcastically : 'This is life, not Peyton Place.'

Rawley confessed : 'My weakness was a younger woman. She was an avaricious, grasping nineteen-year-old go-go dancer.'

'Oh yes, the younger woman – typical case,' Lennie said understandingly.

'One sees it happen so many times to colleagues. What

is it – some middle-aged madness that affects us all? When I first met her, she seemed a sweet young thing. Then over the years, she demanded more and more. Trinkets, trips abroad, a car, a maisonette in South Kensington.'

'I was wrong,' I said sardonically. 'This *is* Peyton Place.'

'How did you meet her?' Lennie asked.

'At our regimental reunion.'

'Oh nice,' I said. 'She was in your regiment, was she?'

'She was part of the cabaret. She was assisting a magician called The Great Alfredo. While he was making cockatoos disappear, my eyes never left Sandra's long, shapely legs.'

'Long and shapely, were they?' Lennie asked wistfully.

'Well, you're paying for those legs now,' I said roughly. 'One glimpse of a young thigh through a fishnet stocking and look at you now.'

Lennie again tried to be diplomatic. 'Well, we're all here because of some form of human weakness. Desire, greed, lust – '

'We're all here, Godber,' I interrupted brusquely, 'because we got caught.'

'All right, but we're all in the same boat. We're all the same under the skin.'

'True. But we don't all wear fishnet tights over it.'

Rawley suddenly asked : 'You'll give me a trial then, Fletcher?'

That tickled me. 'You mean one good trial deserves another? Oh, all right, why not? Like the kid says, we're only flesh and blood. Could work out. I remember in the army they put a rich kid in our billet. He'd been to the best schools. Had all the privileges we so sadly lacked. And suddenly there he was with a bunch of strangers. In fact, in the next bed to him was Alfie Wright, who'd been the leader of one of the biggest gangs of Teds in South London – a real hard case. Well, we treated the rich kid just like everyone else, and you know what? Every week when his daddy's allowance come, he shared it with the rest of us.'

'He did?' Rawley asked wonderingly.

'Yeah. If he hadn't, Alfie would have stove his head in. Good night, your honour.'

The next morning, as I scrubbed the old Hampsteads, I caught sight of Rawley's toilet sundries spread out before me. I rinsed, spat, marked my tube and then commented :

'You can tell we have the upper classes with us. Have you had a butcher's at these toiletries, Len? Mustang talc for men. Rave d'Armour shaving cream. And exhibit C, a badger's hair shaving brush. My God, no wonder you never see a badger these days.'

Lennie attempted to deflect my sarcasm. 'Nocturnal animal, the badger.'

'What?'

'Nocturnal. Only comes out at night.'

'Course they do. They've learnt their lesson, haven't they? If they come out during the day, people make shaving brushes out of them.'

Rawley said deferentially, 'You're more than welcome to use any of my things.'

'No, thank you. And *you* better not use them either, if you know what's good for you.'

'Why?'

'Any idea what effect Mustang will have on the fairies in here?'

There was the harsh sound of bolts being withdrawn. The door creaked open and the hideous, yellow-fanged face of MacKay intruded.

'Good morning, Rawley. How did you sleep?'

'Oh, listen to this,' I exclaimed bitterly. 'All the time I been inside you never asked me how I slept.'

'I know how you sleep, Fletcher. You sleep soundly because you have no conscience, no shame, no guilt.'

'All the things which explain my sleepless night,' Rawley said miserably.

MacKay said briskly : 'You'll have the weekend to settle in. It's Saturday today and you will stop work at noon. Then the rest of the day is your own.'

'I'll take you to the football match if you like,' Lennie offered.

'I'm quite prepared to work on. Helps kill the time.'

'Here,' I protested, 'if you wants to be one of us, you knocks off when we knocks off.'

'Typical prison mentality,' MacKay sneered.

'Wrong. Typical working-class mentality.'

He chuckled evilly. 'Are you saying you consider yourself *working* class, Fletcher?'

'Well, I always used to. Till I went to Glasgow one time. Then I realised I was middle class.'

'That'll be enough, Fletcher !'

Rawley, struggling to blend with his new background, explained : 'All I meant was I rather enjoyed the work you assigned me to.'

I observed : 'Of course you do. Central records. Privilege, that is.'

'No, it's not, Fletcher,' MacKay snapped.

'What, are you saying it's not one of the cushiest numbers in this nick?'

'No, I admit that. But that does not mean it's a privilege.'

'Well, which would you rather do, Mr MacKay, Central Records or latrine duty? Can't sit and read in the latrines, can you? Well, you can but it gets boring reading : now wash your hands, over and over. But Rawley here : one day inside and he scores a job most trustees don't get.'

'He's an educated man. Isn't it logical we should give him a job which requires a clerical aptitude?'

'And since when has logic had anything to do with job allocation? Who was making the blancmange in the canteen yesterday? Riggs, and he's in here for poisoning.'

'Is he?' asked Lennie uneasily.

'Certainly. Cause celebre he was in his home town of Ashton-under-Lyme. Most of his in-laws are under lime now.'

'Is that why they call him arsenic Riggs?'

'No, that's because he once sat on a razor-blade, you nurk.'

MacKay said to Rawley: 'I'm sorry, Rawley, that you're forced to share a cell with riff-raff.'

Rawley said hastily : 'No, they've been most kind and considerate.'

'I hope so. Because I'm aware of the situation, Fletcher, between you and ex-Justice Rawley. But there will be no malice. No vindictiveness. No grudges borne from bitter memory.'

'Grudge? How could I bear a grudge? What has this man ever done to me – except rob me of the best five years of my life?'

With which parting shot I turned and stormed out of the dell.

That afternoon, I breezed into the day room with a copy of *Hare and Hounds,* which I'd just liberated from the screws' common room, under my arm. This periodical was not for reading, since I am not a devotee of the chase, although occasionally a victim of it, but for swapping with a con called Knapton for snout. This Knapton used to be a game warden before he was apprehended in Southampton trying to flog hides to sailors. However,

Knapton proved to be absent. In fact, very few cons were there but those few were arranged in a way which immediately attracted my attention. Four of them – McLaren, Harris and two louts from B Block – were formed in a ring around Rawley who was looking from one to the other of them in a terrified kind of way. Sussing the situation at once, I exclaimed loudly :

'Hello, hello, what's this then? Gunfight at the O.K. Corral?'

Slimy Harris squealed : 'No need to bother yourself, Fletch.'

I replied smoothly : 'Oh, but I do bother, my son. This is my cell block and I'm a long-time resident. And I can tell when something's up.'

McLaren said over his shoulder, while continuing to close in on Rawley : 'He's got it coming, Fletch. And you'll be a prime suspect when he gets it, as he's about to. So get yourself across the yard and out of harm's way. We're doing you a favour, man.'

'Are you about to inflict damage on my cellmate?' I asked.

'Your what?' asked Harris incredulously.

'My cellmate. The bloke with which I share a cell.'

McLaren, still advancing, growled : 'He's no friend of yours.'

'He don't have to be a friend. But he's one of us now, and we looks after our own, don't we?'

McLaren ceased stalking and turned to me with a puzzled glance. 'What are you saying, Fletch?'

'I'm just saying if you takes him on, you takes me on and all. And don't be misled by this bulky torso. It conceals muscles of steel.'

They gaped at me. Then Harris waved something that looked like a deformed butter knife and which he'd probably run up in handicrafts.

'I've got a blade, Fletch.'

'Yeah, well, you'd need one, wouldn't you, Harris? I on the other hand have this rather large volume with which I would happily knock your brains out – if only you had some.'

McLaren sighed. 'Fletch, you're my mate. I don't want to mix it with you.'

'I was banking on that. I hoped that reason and common sense would prevail over your Celtic passion for mayhem and violence.' Judging the moment was right, I said steadily to Rawley : 'On your way, judge.'

He asked nervously, 'On my way where?'

'Out into the yard. Go and watch the football. The word'll go round. No one will lay a finger on you.'

He nodded gratefully and slipped away. Harris brandished his knife in frustration and whined : 'That's a naffing turn-up.'

McLaren said : 'If Fletch wants it that way, that's it. But I would just like to know why. Fletch, what are you doing siding with the establishment?'

'You knows me better than that. It's just that I uses me head. D'you know what this is?' And I held up the large volume I was carrying and winked meaningfully at them.

'What? What?' asked Harris.

'No, not "what, what" – "Who's Who". Now, I've been looking up Rawley. And checking it against the Governor's entry. You want to know something? They only went to the same school, were in the same regiment and belong to the same club. They're life-long bleeding oppos, those two.'

Harris, who has the lightning intellect of a tortoise, wailed : 'That makes it worse.'

'Does it really? Do we whet our appetite for blood or do we agree that what this cell block has always lacked is a life-long friend of the Governor's? Well, Harris, which?'

He gazed at me with furrowed brow. And then, although his eyes did not fill with a wild surmise, a faint nodding of the head made me suspect some glimmer of understanding might be getting through. The others stared at me with respect verging on awe. Then Harris suddenly got the full beauty of it and squealed with delight. Or maybe it was because I'd just dropped "Who's Who" on his foot.

That night, at bedtime, I leaned over the recumbent judge. 'Comfy, your honour? Want another pillow?'

The nurk accepted it and eased it behind his judicial head. 'Oh, thank you.'

'Extra blanket?'

'No, thank you. I'm warm enough.'

'If you're scared of the cockroaches, we can take turns watching out for them,' Lennie contributed.

'You're both very kind. And let me say again, Fletcher, how much I appreciate what you did for me.'

'S'all right. A man in here has a right to prove himself.'

Lennie, sounding faintly aggrieved, protested : 'Here. I said that first.'

'Yeah, but you got it from me, didn't you?'

Rawley said emotionally : 'You, more than anyone, Fletcher, had every right to despise me.'

'No point in that, your worship. No, you just lie back and reminisce about happier times. Tell us about you and the Governor, for example. That should while away a few hours.'

A faint note of caution entered his voice. 'Myself and the Governor?'

I kept it casual. 'Didn't I hear something somewhere that you once knew each other? Or something?'

'Oh, we've known each other for years.'

Lennie said, with assumed innocence, 'What a coincidence.'

Rawley looked from one to the other of us with dawning suspicion. 'I hope this doesn't explain your change of attitude, Fletcher.'

'What?'

'I trust you're not hoping to profit from my past relationship with Geo – with the Governor. Because I must warn you that anything I know about him is in the strictest confidence.'

His tone displeased me. 'Is that so? I'll have me pillow back then.' And I relieved him of it and started to undress.

Rawley sighed and said : 'Fletcher.'

'What?'

'I *am* grateful. I do appreciate what you did today.'

I kept my voice haughty. 'Not all that grateful obviously.'

Whereupon the amazing nurk extended an arm from his pit and invited : 'Shake?'

'What?'

'Shake.'

'Shake what?'

'Hands. No hard feelings, that sort of thing.'

'Why should I have any hard feelings? You're only the bloke that put me in here.'

'Fletcher, I had no choice,' Rawley pleaded.

'Course you did. Several. You could have rejected the jury's verdict. Ordered a retrial. Given me a suspended sentence. Probation. Bound me over.'

'Not in the face of the evidence.'

'And not,' Lennie added, 'with your record, Fletch.'

I thought this over for a moment and then nodded.'I suppose you're right. But if only I'd known then what I know now.'

Rawley sounded pleased. He said, 'Oh, that is reassuring.'

'What is?' I asked.

'Remorse.'

I leaned over him and my eyes bored into his.

'Remorse? It's nothing to do with remorse. It's just that if I'd known you was bent, I'd have made you an offer you wouldn't have refused. Happy dreams, your honour.'

Rough Justice

I looked up from the letter I was writing and asked:
'What d'you want, Warren?'

The thing is, I had me back to the door. So how did
I know who it was? Puzzles me sometimes. Can it be
that your incarcerated male develops some incredible
sixth sense which enables him to perceive psychic vibra-
tions undetectable to the free citizen? Or is it just that
Bunny has a strong pong? Any old how, I was right, as
the piping voice from behind me confirmed.

'I need a letter written. Home like.'

I sighed and turned. 'Warren, how long have you been
inside?'

'Nigh on ten months now.'

'Well, don't you think you'd have been well advised to
take advantage of the educational facilities here and got
rid of your illiteracy?'

'I'm not illiterate, Fletch.'

I saw no point in sparing the sarcasm. 'Forgive me, I
thought that was the word what described someone who
can't read or write.'

'I'm not illiterate. I suffer from dyslexia.'

Could this, I asked myself, account for the pong?

Bunny jeered: 'You don't know what that means, do
you?'

Honour was at stake. I said carefully: 'It's an offensive
condition connected with acid stomach. But I can see no
reason why it should stop you reading or writing.'

Bunny shook his head vigorously. 'Nothing like. Dyslexia is word blindness. I can't identify words on the

written page. They all get jumbled up in my head, you see.'

'Oh yes? Well there's plenty of room, ain't there?'

'Tragic really. If they'd diagnosed it when I were a lad, I wouldn't be in here now.'

'Oh, here we go. The customary alibi. The hard-luck story.'

'It's true in my case. I had a real tough break. You see, I couldn't read the sign.'

'What sign was this?'

'The one that said : "Warning – Burglar Alarm".'

I shook my head sadly. 'That's much the same excuse as Charlie Dill. He's that burglar in B Wing.'

'How?'

'He's deaf. He didn't hear the dog.'

'Really? I didn't know he were short of hearing.'

'That ain't all he's short of since that Airedale got him.'

Bunny glanced about moodily and retreated towards the door, 'I'll come back later.'

I said quickly : 'No, hang about. I'll do it for you. Usual rates. Half-a-snout a page.'

Warren shook his head vigorously. 'No, I weren't going to ask you.'

This was both displeasing and surprising. 'What do you mean?' I asked.

'I were going to ask your new celly, Judge Rawley.'

My indignation immediately rose. 'Why?'

'Take advantage like. He's a judge. Educated man. Oxford. Public school.'

'Oh, I see.' I shook my head bitterly. 'Suddenly bowled over by his worship's academic pedigree, you've dispensed with my literary services, have you?'

'No offence, like. I just thought he has to be the best person for the job.'

I felt that a little correcting of perspective was in order.

'Bunny, letter-writing is an art. A gift. What sort of love letter is he going to write? "My dear Carol, I am in receipt of your letter of the sixth inst., wherebeit I, the undersigned, heretoforward to be referred to as the party of the first part," and so on. He'd be all right if you want to sue her, not woo her.'

This happy phrase, as it seemed to me, had some effect on Warren. He hesitated. 'Well, I just thought – '

Naturally, I pressed my advantage. 'You just thought wrong as usual. Letter writing is a creative art, endowed only to a few of us. I mean, how many of you nurks in here have my poetic turn of phrase? For example, here's what I'm writing to my nearest and dearest. Just read that. Oh, you can't, can you?' With which, I took up my newly-completed epistle and read to him. 'My Darling, though we have been driven apart by cruel fate, and an inexcusable misdirecting of a jury by a biased judge, who is now sharing a cell with me, I know that our love transcends these grey, grim walls that have driven us apart. You are with me in my heart and this knowledge helps me to wring a few drops of comfort from the limp, damp towel of life. Kiss the baby for me, your own Norman.'

Warren, I was gratified to see, seemed impressed. 'Oh, that's beautiful, Fletch,' he exclaimed.

'Yeah, well – '

'I'm sorry, Fletch. Will you do a letter for me? When you've got a moment?'

I nodded distantly. Now that I'd got him hooked, it would be bad policy to seem too eager. 'When I've got a moment, yes. But first I've got to finish this one off and get it sent. After that, I've got to write one to the wife.'

A faint odour of expensive after-shave wafted into the dell. It was closely followed by Judge Rawley.

'Oh, good evening, Warren,' he said pleasantly.

Warren, as is his nature, immediately cringed. 'Oh, hello, judge. Your honour.' He bowed.

I said testily, 'Don't call him that. Don't smarm up to him. He is not a judge. He is a former judge, an ex-judge. He has been debenched or you might say dewigged.'

Warren shook his head dubiously. 'He's pending appeal, and you never know – '

With which, Warren prepared to take his departure. Rawley detained him. 'Oh, Warren, that matter you raised with me in the canteen. I'll give it a little thought and speak to you in the morning.'

'Oh, thank you, Judge. Night, Fletch.'

And he and his dyslexia departed.

'What little matter was this then?' I asked.

'Oh, just a legal matter. Something to do with his sister's tenancy of her council house.'

'Oh, I see. Setting up shop, are we?'

'Excuse me?'

'Steven Rawley, Q.C., is now open for business? What you charging then?'

'I'm not charging anything.'

I clicked disapprovingly. 'Well, that's daft to start with. If you have any expertise in here which is in demand, then it's saleable. Rule of the house. It's expected. And any philanthropic notions will be taken as a sign of weakness.'

Rawley seemed taken aback by these nick truths. 'I didn't realise – '

'No, well you ain't got the acumen. I'll work out your fees. We'll split 'em fifty-fifty.'

He drew himself up until his shiny pate nearly reached my chin. 'I have no intention – '

I broke in roughly. 'You will do.'

'I will not.'

He was bent but he might not scare easy. I tried persuasion. 'Listen, we could clean up. I mean, there's six hundred blokes in here, all of whom has a legal gripe. We do have an ex-solicitor across the block but he only knows about mortgages and there's not a lot of call for that in here. One thing we *are* sure of is a roof over our head. I tell you where we *could* score heavy. All the poofs in here are getting a movement together. You know, "Equal rights for Homosexuals". You're the perfect man to represent them. Queen's Counsel, ain't you?'

'I am not hawking my legal expertise to the highest bidder.'

'No need to. I do the hawking. You just dispense.'

'Out of the question. I would be mad to engage in anything of that nature until I hear the result of my appeal. Within a month I could be back on the bench. One has to preserve some sort of integrity.'

I sniffed. 'Oh, integrity, is it? I love your high moral tone, despite the disgrace you've wrought on your profession. Do get it into your head, you're now inside. Another world. It's a jungle in here. And you just happen to be fortunate enough to be sharing a cage with King Kong.'

But he stuck to his guns and in the end I let it go – for the time being.

Strange how things go in pairs, ain't it? I'd recognise Warren without seeing him and later that very day, Lennie, as he told me afterwards, had the same experience with Harris. Lennie was alone in the flowery at the time working on a model aeroplane. Why that lad's always making extra work for himself beats me but if it's not Spanish or boxing it's model-making. Anyway, he was just gluing on a fin or something when there was a horrible change in the atmosphere. Now that I come to think of it, Lennie's experience was not identical with mine. It wasn't that he recognised Harris by his pong but that he recoiled from him.

'Is that you?' Lennie gasped.

'Me what?' asked Harris.

'That pong.'

'There's a reason for this pong.'

'There'd have to be. And for your sake I hope it's curable.'

Harris said peevishly, 'They've moved me back on the naffing farm, haven't they?'

'Nice job that. Lots of exercise. Fresh air.'

'Fresh air?' echoed Harris incredulously. 'I'm swilling out the flaming pigs. You know why, don't you?'

Lennie considered it. 'Well, they try to fit people to their most appropriate function. You and pigs – that makes sense.'

'Watch your lip, Godber.'

Lennie protruded it but the task proved beyond him.

'I'll tell you why I'm on the farm,' Harris snorted. ' 'Cause they've been rejigging jobs round here. To accommodate your naffing V.I.P.'

'Judge Rawley?'

'That's him. And he only went straight into a clerk's job. Trustee's by right.'

Lennie, engrossed in his model building, ignored this. He mused aloud. 'Has its advantages though, the farm. Don't you get outside trips, like?'

'Oh yes,' grunted Harris bitterly. 'Only today I went for a trip in the back of a pig truck that hadn't been cleaned for three weeks, slipping about inside. We picked up six new pigs and clipped back only just in time for supper.'

'Couldn't you have had a bath?'

'This is what I smell like after a bath.'

'But didn't you see anything or anybody?'

'Yes. I'm forgetting the highlight of the day. I caught a glimpse of a woman.'

Lennie whistled. 'A female woman, really? What was she like?'

Harris shook his head in wonderment. 'Well, porridge does strange things to a man. It's the first time I've been turned on by a fifteen-stone pig-breeder.'

At this point, Warren and I arrived at the dell. The discovery that it was being polluted by one of the least savoury inhabitants of the nick did nothing for my temper. I growled, 'What are you on, Harris?'

'Social call,' he replied breezily.

Something hit me. I gasped and wrinkled my nose. 'Dear me, what's that smell?'

'Put me back on the pig farm, didn't they?'

'Yeah. I heard the pigs held a protest march. At least it takes away the smell of Godber's aeroplane glue.'

Warren, to my surprise, had been delicately sipping the air as though it was an unfamiliar but attractive vintage. He said appreciatively, 'I quite like the smell. It reminds me of home.'

'Born on a farm, was you?' I asked.

'No,' said Warren.

I turned back to the Great Pong. 'Clear off, Harris, go on. It's beginning to smell like a Turkish restaurant in here.'

Harris tried a feeble counter-attack. 'If this cell stinks, it's because of His Worship. Don't know how you stomach a bloke like that.'

But I waved him away irritably. 'On your way, Harris.'

He edged towards the door. Then, like a schoolboy, he called back as he darted away : 'We'll have him, you know. In the end, we'll have him.'

I looked after him, shaking my head, and murmured : 'Charmless nurk.'

Lennie suddenly swivelled round and cried : 'Has he whipped my aerofix?' But then his hand encountered it under some diagrams. 'Oh no, here it is.'

He resumed work. I said, with mild reproach, 'I'd be glad if you wouldn't leave that aerofix lying about, Godber. I came back last week from the shower and sat on it unbeknownst. An hour later, I had to be prized out of me underpants. Talk about a stiff upper lip.'

Warren nodded impatiently and said : 'Come on, then, Fletch, let's have me letter.'

'Let's see the snout first, then.'

Warren duly produced the agreed number of fags and, in return, I produced an envelope from under the pillow on my bunk. Bunny asked eagerly : 'Is it good?'

'It's inspired, my son.'

'You reckon Elaine will like it?'

'No question. Did you happen to notice that last night on the box, after our bedtime naturally, they was showing an old Rita Hayworth film? Well, it was called "Fire Down Below". That, my son, is exactly what your Elaine will feel when she reads this.'

Godber, who has large gaps in his education, asked : 'Who was Rita Hayworth?'

'Gawd, Godber, you are ignorant.'

He said cheerfully, 'No, I'm just young.'

'And you missed out, my son. Your deprived generation – what have you got? Twiggy and Tatum O'Neill.'

But Lennie said smugly : 'Since the Olympics, my sexual fantasies are mostly East European gymnasts.'

I smiled pityingly. 'I'm talking about *women*, my son. Your Rhonda Flemings, your Virginia Mayos. And at the top of that glorious heap of pulchritude was always – my Rita.'

'Your favourite, was she?' asked Lennie, peering at the letter.

'Still is.'

'And is that why you've put Dear Rita instead of Dear Elaine?'

I snatched up the letter. 'Have I? Oh well, lend us your pen.'

I was about to cross out the offending name when Warren protested : ' 'Ere, that's not going to look nice. She'll think I've got a Rita on me mind. She'll get jealous.'

There was justice in this. I sighed. 'Okay, Bunny, I'll copy it again for you later.'

At this point we all became aware of a kind of quiver in the air. It was like what happens in courts of justice when the bewigged magistrate is approaching and everyone prepares to leap to his feet in respect. Sure enough, a moment later Rawley strode into the dell. He was not wearing his wig and gown but nevertheless there was something imposing about him. He glanced at us briskly and said : 'Good evening.'

We returned the salutation. As he stowed his washing gear, Rawley remarked : 'In the showers, I ran across that chap from Liverpool – what's his name?'

'Harris?' Lennie suggested.

'Harris, yes. He was most abusive.'

'Take no notice of Harris,' I urged.

'But he threatened me.'

'He's all wind and water,' I explained. 'You know what he's in for, don't you? Snatching an old-age pensioner's handbag.'

'He never !' exclaimed Bunny.

'At least, he tried to,' I continued smoothly. 'She pinned him down till the cops arrived. She kept hitting him over the head with her handbag.'

Rawley looked puzzled. 'And that subdued him, you say?'

'Not half – it had a brick in it. She was on her way to do a smash-and-grab.'

'Good grief,' exclaimed the former judge.

'Don't you worry, your honour,' Lennie said encouragingly. 'If anyone comes on strong, you know we'll always back you up.'

'Yeah, we'll see you all right,' I grunted.

Rawley gazed from one to the other of us, and then said feelingly : 'You already have. I'm most grateful. You men have every right to despise me. Especially you, Fletcher, since I sent you here in the first place. But you have all shown me only kindness, compassion and sympathy. I feel a bond with you men which I know has been forged in adversity, but I think will remain with me always.'

Now this was far from your normal rabbit-and-pork in the nick where any remark more tender than 'shut your face' is likely to be regarded as an emotional outburst. We shuffled uncomfortably and I muttered : ' 'Ere, leave it off, judge. If you go on like this, you're going to make us forget our scruples and like you.'

But there was no holding him. 'I mean it. Who'd have thought a few months ago that I could so much as talk to you. Now I find that I respect you. More than that – I trust you.'

Lennie gulped and I wouldn't swear he didn't flick faintly at the corner of his eye. 'You mean that?' he asked.

'Most sincerely.' And then, possibly to spare us embarrassment, Rawley turned back to his gear. Almost immediately, he said sharply : 'Just a moment.'

'What's up?' asked Lennie.

Rawley turned back and confronted us. His voice was steely. 'Which one of you stole my watch?'

'Your what?' I asked in astonishment.

'My watch. It was there when I went to the showers and it's not there now.'

Lennie was outraged. 'Here, hold your horses. What's happened to that most sincere trust you felt for us?'

'That was before one of you stole my watch.'

This was coming it a bit strong. I moved up for a nose-to-nose confrontation and said : ' 'Ere, 'ere, 'ere, you'd better back off, your worship. We don't rip each other off. We're mates, oppos. We have a code.'

Rawley smiled grimly. 'But I'm still an outsider.'

I shrugged. 'That's true. Give him his watch, Len.'

'That's not funny, Fletch,' protested Lennie. 'I'm no petty sneak thief. Give him his watch, Warren.'

'Pardon?' blinked Bunny. 'I haven't got his naffing watch. I only come in for me letter, which I haven't had read to me yet.'

Whereupon Lennie said reproachfully to Rawley : 'See what you've done, judge? Stirred up mistrust among people who trust each other implictly. Go on, Fletch, give him his watch.'

I said silkily : 'You talking to me like that, Godber? You watch it, my son, or I'll darken your outlook.'

At this, Rawley burst out apologetically. 'I'm sorry. I'm sorry. I was being stupidly hasty. My legal training should have prevented me from making accusations without firm evidence.'

'Never bothered the law in my hometown,' muttered Bunny.

Rawley continued : 'But I swear to you, my watch *was* there when I went to take my shower.'

I saw the answer. 'Harris ! How long was he here before I came in?'

'Long enough,' confirmed Lennie. 'He could have palmed it when I was glueing this aileron on.'

'Come on, then,' urged Warren, 'let's gerrafter him.'

I raised a restraining hand. 'Hold on, hold on, you know the crafty git will have stashed it by now.'

The piercing note of the bell which announces lock-up sounded. 'Timed his exit well and all,' Lennie observed. 'Can't go nowhere now.'

'I'll have to be off home, Fletch,' said Bunny. 'Should I not say nowt?'

I nodded. 'Yeah. Shtum, Warren.'

'Should we get him tomorrow, then, and extract a confession somewhere where his screams won't be heard?'

There was a gasp from Rawley. 'Oh no, please!' he begged. 'I've already acted irrationally. I beg you not to do the same. We have no proof –'

I cut him short. 'Just a minute, your honour, d'you mind?' I turned to Warren. 'Okay, Bunny. Saturday tomorrow, football, visitors, lot of diversions. We'll need a quiet room, but we'll also need an eye-out, won't we? Tell you what, ask Frankie Lovelace and Percy the Wrench if they want to make a bob or two.'

'O.K.,' agreed Warren. 'Good night all.'

He scampered off. Rawley, looking dazed, repeated : 'Percy the Wrench?'

I reassured him. 'It's all right. We only want them as minders.'

'But we cannot take the law into our own hands. I shall report the theft to the proper channels.'

I pointed out : 'In here, we are the proper channels. And we looks after our own.'

'Even if "our own" was as impulsively accusatory as what you were,' Lennie added.

Rawley shook his head sadly. 'I've told you, I regret that. And I don't want you people acting in the same impulsive manner.'

'Calm down,' I said soothingly. 'We ain't going to set upon Harris. We're going to conduct a civilised investigation. We're all familiar with the workings of the law, and we're fortunate in this instance to have a guest judge.'

'Guest judge?' asked Rawley, who seemed a bit slow on the uptake.

I elaborated. 'A member of that noble profession what you so recently besmirched. On the other hand, you do know your law.'

'You mean,' asked Rawley doubtfully, 'we're going to have a hearing?'

'A trial, my son.'

'But do we have enough to go on?'

Lennie explained. 'Yes. Harris's reputation.'

Rawley frowned. 'I know he's objectionable, but is he a known thief?'

I rebuked him. 'You should know better than to ask that. We might tell you things which would prejudice your impartiality, know what I mean?'

'Innocent till proven guilty, like,' Lennie offered.

Rawley said hastily, 'Of course. Of course. The less I know about Harris the better.'

'That's right,' I encouraged him. 'Why should you want to know about him? A despicable nurk that would sell his Granny's wintergreen.' I noticed Rawley shaking his head disapprovingly. 'Oh, sorry – let that be stricken from the record, your honour.'

As we started undressing for bed, Lennie asked : 'Are you going to prosecute, Fletch?'

'Certainly. Should be interesting seeing the other side of the fence, like.'

'But,' asked Rawley, 'do you know enough about legal procedure?'

I laughed mirthlessly. 'Been up enough, ain't I? Look, when you choose your living breaking the law, it pays to know the laws you're bleeding breaking. And I've had enough first-hand experience with counsels. Clever men, most of them. Although my last one weren't too bright, as my presence in this nick indicates.'

Rawley cleared his throat and then said hesitantly: 'As the presiding judge at your trial, Fletcher, I thought your counsel argued eloquently against impossible odds.'

I heard Lennie titter.

'Godber!' I warned. Then I turned back to Rawley. 'Listen, my counsel was a loser going in. And I ain't referring to the evidence. I'm talking about his attitude. Before the trial, he comes to see me in Brixton, doesn't he? And you know what the pompous git says? I couldn't believe it.'

'What?' asked Lennie.

I delivered it in the wig-in-the-mouth voice all them barristers use. ' "I should like you to know that myself and my staff shall dispose ourselves with the utmost vigour and dedication in refuting the charges against you. Investigators will pursue a tenacious enquiry into unearthing evidence and testimony. Researchers will work into the night assembling and collating the facts at our disposal, on which I shall marshall a defence which has left no stone unturned, no avenue unexplored and which will culminate in your honourable and justifiable release. In the meantime, please proceed with your escape plan." '

The next day, court was convened in the B Wing boiler room. This place had not been designed with trials in view and a certain amount of improvisation proved necessary. We smuggled in a table and some chairs and shovelled the coke into a heap against the wall.

Rawley gazed about miserably at his new court-room. He commented: 'This is most irregular. I cannot say I'm happy about these proceedings, Fletcher.'

'Yeah, well, happiness is relative, isn't it?' I pointed

out. 'I mean, this is nick. Who's happy, know what I mean?'

Lennie gestured deferentially towards the table and asked: 'Would you like to assume your customary seat behind the bench, your honour?'

As Rawley hesitated, I urged, 'Go on, park your backside.'

Lennie said, 'We should have got him a wig.'

'We could have borrowed one from one of the Transylvanians in here,' said Warren.

I clicked reprovingly. 'The word, Warren, is transvestite. You are a nurk, ain't you? A Transylvanian is someone in a horror film.'

'Which describes most of this nick's transvestites,' Lennie pointed out.

'All right, smarty, but there's nothing very judicial about a platinum blonde wig shaped like a bleeding beehive, is there? Because that is what your ambidexterers wear round here.'

Warren, who was minding at the door, hissed: 'Hey up – here comes the accused.'

'Under escort is he?' I asked.

Warren nodded. 'Yeah. Black Jock's got him in a half nelson.'

I prodded Rawley, who still did not seem completely reconciled to the judicial proceedings. 'Do sit down, your honour. Court is convened.'

As he did so, Harris stumbled into the chamber in the vice-like grip of McLaren. As soon as he saw us, the defendant burst out: 'Here, here, what's going on then? You got no flaming right –'

'Silence in court!' I bellowed in his ear.

'What?'

'Harris, sit down.' McLaren dumped him in a chair. 'Now, Harris, as the prisoner at the bar you are entitled to know what these proceedings are in aid of. We are here to pursue the course of justice and find you guilty.'

There was a groan from the bench. 'Fletcher, please,' protested Rawley.

Lennie said quickly, 'None of us heard that. Well, if we did, it's stricken from our minds.'

Harris bleated : 'What is?'

'The fact that you're guilty.'

'Here, listen – '

I cut in swiftly : 'No, you listen, Harris. A watch has disappeared from our flowery dell, and you are the prime suspect.'

'Why me?'

'Because otherwise it's us and we're above suspicion. Right?'

'No, it's not flaming right – '

But McLaren shook the reptile, snarling : 'Shut up, you.'

Rawley bobbed to his feet and said in a strained voice : 'I must protest these – '

I waved him silent. 'All right, your honour, d'you mind? Thank you. Now, Harris, let me put your mind at rest. You shall get a fair trial. We have a qualified Judge with a long, though slightly blemished, record. We have an eye-witness.'

'Who?' asked Harris.

'Me,' replied Lennie.

I promised : 'And I am going to prosecute you. But to ensure absolute fair play, you will be defended.'

'Oh?'

'By Warren.'

'By Warren?' moaned Harris.

'What's wrong with that?' asked Bunny.

Harris pointed a finger at his new counsel but addressed the rest of us. 'He's flaming illiterate, he is.'

'He is not,' I corrected him. It is a medically-proven fact that Warren is – er – is – '

'Dyslectic,' supplied Warren.

'That's it. Dyslectic.'

Lennie said interestedly, 'I never knew that.'

Warren smiled modestly. 'Yes, for years.'

'Really? Is it contagious?'

I intervened irritably. 'For Gawd's sake, Godber, we're in a court of law.'

'Sorry, Fletch.'

Harris tried again to get his say in. ' 'Ere, listen – '

'Shut up!' urged McLaren menacingly.

'Doesn't a man have a right to speak?' demanded Harris.

I explained. 'Certainly. But in your case only when spoken to.' Then, using cunning forensic skill, I asked him : 'If you're innocent, what you in such a state about?'

'You ask me that – with Warren defending me?'

Warren felt it desirable to set the record straight. 'Here, Harris, I didn't volunteer for the job. I don't like you.'

Harris appealed bitterly to Judge Rawley. 'D'you hear this? D'you hear this?'

I said judiciously, 'It's all right, Harris. He don't have to like you to defend you. You think any of our counsels liked us?'

Lennie nodded approvingly. 'That's a good point, that is.'

'Right, Harris,' I said briskly, 'how do you plead?'

'Excuse me, Fletcher?' Rawley said desperately.

'What? Oh yes, be my guest, your honour.'

'All right then, Harris,' said Rawley to the suspect, 'how do you plead? Guilty or Not Guilty?'

'Not guilty,' affirmed Harris.

I commented sadly, 'I see – a liar as well as a thief.'

Warren called : 'Objection !'

We looked at him in some surprise, never having suspected that there might be a legal eagle buried in Bunny.

Rawley encouraged him : 'All right then, Warren, go on. What is your objection?'

Warren gazed at us blankly, his brow furrowed. Finally, he stammered, 'Er – I don't know.'

Harris prompted desperately : 'Flaming heck. You were objecting to the fact that I was called a liar and a thief.'

But Bunny shook his head resolutely. 'No, I wasn't. We all know you're a liar and a thief, Harris.'

Rawley said sternly : 'That remark should be struck from the record.'

'Unnecessary,' I pointed out, 'since there ain't no record. Now I'd like to call my first and only witness, Leonard Arthur Godber. Take the stand, would you, please.'

Lennie advanced. 'I swear to tell the truth, the whole – '

'Never mind that,' I remonstrated. 'We've got about ten minutes before the screws tumble us. Just tell us about the events of last night, Mr Godber.'

'Well, Mr Rawley took his watch off prior to going to the showers. At the time I was in our cell utilising my spare time in a constructive manner, to wit making a flying fortress. Harris come in. Then Mr Fletcher and the defending counsel entered the room, telling the accused to naff off, which he promptly did. Shortly afterwards, the watch was found not to be there and has not been seen since.'

Rawley turned to Warren, in a very official tone of voice : 'Counsel for the Defence – that's you, Warren – do you wish to cross-examine this witness?'

'Pardon?' asked Bunny.

'Do you wish to ask him any questions?'

'No, I were there. I know what happened.'

'Flaming heck,' moaned Harris, whereupon McLaren shook him again.

Rawley pronounced: 'Let him speak. He has that right.'

'Ta, judge,' said Harris. 'Now, you all know as well as me that this is a mockery. You know as well as me that all this is flaming hearsay. No one can prove nowt. Like, where's the evidence?'

Rawley nodded. 'I have to agree with him. One man's word against another's does not constitute legal evidence. This case would not stand up in a Court of Law, upon which these proceedings are supposedly modelling themselves. In the absence of evidence, there is no prima facie case and I am forced to dismiss the accused.'

Harris beamed. 'Thank you, your honour.'

'Now, hang about, Judge,' I urged. 'Who's side are you on?'

'I'm sorry, Fletcher,' apologised Rawley, 'but you insisted on a proper enquiry.'

McLaren, frustrated by these legal thickets, asked: 'Would a signed confession help?'

'Do we have one?' asked Rawley in surprise.

'I could soon get one.'

'He's threatening me!' Harris squealed.

'Good Lord,' exclaimed Rawley, 'I must protest at this intimidation – '

'Judge!' I said firmly, 'it's best you stay out of this, know what I mean?' I turned to Harris. 'Harris, we don't want no unpleasantness. So wherever you stashed the watch, go dig it out. All right? If you traded it, go trade it back. We just wants that watch back. If not, the consequences to your good self are too dire to contemplate.'

Harris gazed around at the grim faces. He asked: 'Have I definitely been found "Not Guilty"?'

I nodded. 'You have.'

'All right,' he agreed. 'I'll go and get it.'

And he did just that.

That evening, when I returned to the cell after taking three snouts off Bunny at dominoes, I found Lennie hard at work on his model.

'Evening, Fletch,' he chirped. 'Look, almost finished.' And he held up a large, but somewhat tatty, model aeroplane.

'Oh yes,' I complimented him, 'very good. How you going to get it in the bottle, then?'

'Going to hang it on the ceiling. When I was a kid I had planes all over me bedroom. Me dad made them. From the war, like. Hurricanes, Spitfires, Mess of Schmidts. That's how I know what shape a Flying Fortress was. Me Dad told me.'

'Pity he didn't tell you about what shape Rita Hayworth and Rhonda Fleming was and all.'

'No, he didn't talk much about women.'

A thought occurred to me. 'Was he all right, your Dad? Not one of them, was he?'

Lennie shook his head. 'He didn't know they existed in them days.'

'Oh yes. Your poofter just wasn't so blatant then. In *my* father's day, they used to horsewhip them, you know. Now they've become fashionable. What worries me is they might make it compulsory.'

I seated myself and withdrew a slightly greasy copy of the *Sun* from my pocket. Lennie asked : 'See his worship?'

'Heard he had a call to see the Governor.'

'What'll that be about?'

'Have to ask him, won't we?'

'Here, you don't think he'll blow the gaff, do you? About our Kangaroo Court?'

'Nah. He's learned we takes care of our own. He'll respect that.'

Lennie nodded. 'Specially since Harris gave him his watch back.'

At this point Rawley breezed into the flowery. He seemed strangely chuffed.

'Good evening, Fletch, Lennie,' he chortled.

'Evening,' returned Lennie politely.

'I'm glad you're both here because I want to thank you, and tell you that I realise now a lot of what you say is true. There are grave abuses of justice. There is often one law for the rich and powerful, and another law for the poor and oppressed. And the poor usually suffer while the rich get off with clever lawyers. But I want to promise you one thing. I shall remember that lesson when I leave here.'

'That won't be for some time, though,' I pointed out.

'Oh no,' he announced cheerfully. 'I'm going out tonight.'

Lennie dropped his model in surprise and I let the *Sun* sink.

'You're what?' asked Lennie. 'Going out?'

'Yes.'

I caught on. 'Your appeal's come through?'

Rawley had already begun to pack. He nodded happily. 'Certainly. I'm rich and powerful. I have clever lawyers.'

Later that evening, in the Association area, we were privileged to hear the last of Judge Rawley's straight-from-the-bleeding-heart addresses. Not only us but quite an assortment of the lads were there. Rawley, elegantly clad in a Judge's streetwear, was ushered in by MacKay.

'All right, you men! The Governor has kindly allowed Mr Rawley to bid you a fond farewell.'

'Oh, it's Mister now, is it?' I muttered.

'Certainly, Fletcher. If the appeal court judges say his nose is clean, that's good enough for me. They are, after all,' MacKay went on haughtily, 'men of the highest integrity in the land.'

'What are you talking about?' I asked. 'He's *one* of them.'

'Precisely. And he's innocent, which proves my point.'

I couldn't think of an answer to that one, and meanwhile Rawley cleared his throat and began :

'Er – Gentlemen, it's just that I wanted to say goodbye and thank you once more, and to promise you something. Whatever I can do to improve the system, I shall do. This has been a frightening experience for me, but, thanks to you men, a rewarding one.'

This effort was received in uneasy silence. Rawley glanced nervously around at the stony faces. I rose and held out my hand.

'Listen,' I assured him, 'you got a break. No one holds that against anybody.'

This broke the ice. There was a murmur of agreement from the lads and even one or two 'hear, hears'. We all crowded round good old Judge Rawley and Warren actually plucked up the courage to slap him on the back. Lennie urged him : 'You behave yourself now. Don't want to see you back, do we?'

Rawley stammered : 'Thank you, thank you – oh, one more thing.' He turned to me. 'Fletcher, I'd like you to have this.'

And he held out the very article which had been the cause of our show trial that afternoon. I shook my head.

'No, I don't want your watch. No need for that. Besides, only reason they allow watches in this nick is to remind us how slowly the time passes.'

Rawley insisted. 'But surely you could trade it? It's valuable.'

This was indeed a telling argument. I took the item from him and nodded. 'Oh, ta very much, then.'

Rawley smiled at us all. 'Once again then, goodbye – my friends.'

And he turned towards freedom. Lennie suddenly had an idea and detained him with the words : 'Here, Judge. When we get out, we'll come and look you up.'

Rawley hesitated and then turned back to us. I added enthusiastically : 'Yeah, talk about old times, re-establish our friendship, meet your family. Why, we could bring our wives round to meet your wife.'

Rawley's jaw dropped slightly. It was easy to see how moved he was by our suggestion. He nodded weakly.

'Yes – yes, indeed. That would be – nice – awfully nice – really – '

Then he turned and fled.

McLaren shook his head. 'Off he goes – free as a bird.'

'And free to go and find himself a bird, and all,' I pointed out.

Lennie sighed. 'While we remain behind to carry on vegetating.'

I could not refute this. 'True, Lennie, true. But I like to think we've all learned a little from his visit, albeit short. I think we may all have gained something as a result.'

'You have,' Lennie agreed. 'You've gained his wrist-watch.'

Bunny Warren said disgustedly, 'Needn't have bothered with that trial. Waste of time.'

'Not in my case. Bunny,' I contradicted him cheer-fully. 'As Lennie so rightly remarked, in my case I have gained time – in the shape of this genuine gold-plated, 14-jewelled gents' wristwatch, in full working – ' but as I said the last words I realised that something about Judge Rawley's gift had been bothering me ever since he'd presented it to me. It lacked the dynamic feel of your true chronometer. It seemed light in the hand. I flipped it over and opened the back. Then I looked up and roared : 'Where's that Harris? I'll murder him ! It's got no bleeding works in it !'

Pardon Me

For fifteen years, old Blanco only had two interests in the nick : Muffin the Mule and Monopoly. Then he put the finishing touches to Muffin the Mule and it was all down to Monopoly. Fearing that his outlook would get narrow, I suggested that he have a go at Donald Duck or even Paddington Bear. But he said there wasn't time. Not for a true artist. Muffin had taken fifteen years to complete. Blanco was a long-server. But even he would be released before another fifteen years had passed. So I urged him to have a go at some less heroic work : Dougal, for example, or perhaps just a simple bust of Mickey Mouse. But Blanco didn't seem to think that, after Muffin, these would prove very satisfying. He greeted the suggestion with scorn, as Christopher Wren might have done if, just after he had supervised the completion of St Paul's, his old lady had asked him to run her up a garden shed.

So we all had to take turns playing Monopoly with Blanco. And it was far from bliss. A nice courteous old con most of the time, over the Monopoly board Blanco turned into a fiend. He played Monopoly the way Stuart Granger — or am I thinking of Cary Grant? — the way one of them played Black Jack in Dodge City — or am I thinking of Stud in Tombstone? Any old how, Blanco played to win. And he wasn't particular how he did it. He was a very good Monopoly player because of long practice. But he supplemented his skill by such ploys as sneaking houses on to his properties when you weren't looking and snaffling up play money. Has to be said : Blanco cheated at

Monopoly. This did not make for a restful game. And for me the only point of playing games in the nick is to relax. So how did I ever get involved in a four-day marathon Monopoly session with Blanco? By the fourth afternoon, we were playing with gimlet eyes fixed on each other and, if we'd been wearing them, our holster flaps would have been unfastened.

'Ha,' I exclaimed, moodily examining a 'chance' card. 'Would you Christmas eve it – "Go to Jail. Go directly to Jail. Do not pass Go, do not collect – ".'

'I know the flaming words,' Blanco snarled. 'Just get on with it.'

A tiny muscle in his jaw twitched. I said, in a level voice, 'It's your toss, isn't it?'

He tossed. I looked at the dice. 'Four and three. Seven.'

'I know,' he growled. 'I can count. I may be old but I've still got all my faculties.'

'Oh, that's lovely,' I complimented him. 'I should be sorry to think you'd lost a couple.'

'What I have lost is a hotel. Pick it up for me, would you, Fletch?'

'Oh, come off it, Blanco. I saw you work that one last week with Godber. He picked up your dice and you snaffled up half of Bond Street and King's Cross while he was doing it.'

Blanco's body stiffened and I saw his hand creep towards his hip. A voice whispered in my head : he's going to make his play – now. But what he came up with was his snuff box. He took a pinch of snuff, shuddered, sneezed and said : 'It's a flaming lie. Listen, Fletch, I'm not like you lot. With you, cheating is a way of life. But I'm an older man with an older man's sense of values, so if you don't care a rat's about my sciatic nerve I'll get the hotel meself.'

With a groan he began to hoist himself up. Naturally, this affected by tender heart. I urged : 'Hey – hey, hang on. I'm sorry, Blanco.'

He sank back in his seat. I continued : 'You're right. We're all so corrupt in here, we forget there's the odd honest soul.'

Then I rose and began to look for his missing hotel. There was a flicker of movement from Blanco's direction which just might have been his hand snaking out for a couple of houses. But I couldn't be sure. I didn't see his hotel anywhere. Then Blanco exclaimed : 'Oh look, there it is.'

He bent down to retrieve the little red building and, simply to keep fair do's with him, I slipped three five-hundred pound notes from the bank onto my pile. Then the game continued.

About an hour later, I heard two familiar voices behind me. The first belonged to Slade Prison's favourite screw, Mr Barrowclough. It asked :

'Are they still playing?'

This exasperated query was answered by an even more familiar voice, that of my cellie, Lennie Godber. He explained soberly : 'Four days now. Could make the Guinness Book of Records.'

'They're cheating each other into a stalemate, that's why.'

Naturally, I bristled at this monstrous allegation. But I couldn't turn round to remonstrate with Barra for fear Blanco would slash my assets. I called : 'What's that, Mr Barrowclough?'

'I said, you two cheat each other into a stalemate.'

My indignation got the better of me. I turned.

'Who says we're cheating? I'm one of this nick's most honest men. And Blanco's an old man with an old man's sense of – I saw that, Blanco !'

I had turned back to the table just in time to see Blanco's hand in the till. He whined : 'I were only changing a hundred-pound note.'

'Yeah, into a flaming five-hundred pound one !'

'An inspiration to us all,' sighed Mr Barrowclough. 'All right, you two. I think it's time you wrapped up this marathon. Lock up in five minutes.'

Lennie said, 'You two do tend to monopolise that game. Get it? Monopolise?'

Barrowclough gazed blankly at Lennie for a moment. Then he caught on. 'Oh – yes – very witty, Godber.'

Lennie shrugged modestly and asked : 'What's brown, lives in the ocean and attacks young mermaids?'

Barrowclough looked uncertain, like a cow inspecting a bunch of plastic flowers. He shook his head. 'I've no idea.'

'Jack the Kipper.'

This background was not helping play. I was about to suggest that they both naff off and leave us to the final shoot-out when someone new arrived in Funland. It was Lukewarm. He immediately set about Blanco.

'Oh, there you are. You're a naughty old person. You promised me you were going to wash your work shirt. So you'd look presentable for Parole Board.'

'I'm going to, aren't I?'

I was conscious of a distinct feeling of irritation. We only had five more minutes to play. Then I had a butcher's at the game. Blanco had made his pile. There was only a tatty ten-pound note left in the bank. How he'd done it I couldn't tell but if it came to a reckoning, it would cost me a deal of snout. So I turned jauntily to Lukewarm.

'Come off it, me old son. Seventeen-year stretch and you think the Parole Board's going to be swayed by a clean shirt? It's his clean record that counts.'

'Silly to jeopardise it for the sake of a drop of soap and water, though,' said Lukewarm.

'I can't come now. I've got two on Piccadilly. I'll come in a minute.'

'See you do.' And Lukewarm slouched off.

'Worse than me daughter, nagging,' Blanco murmured.

'I thought he was your daughter,' I said.

'Still, he does keep the cell spotless.'

'Well, you soon won't have to worry about that. You're on your way out, aren't you?'

Lennie nodded sagely. 'You're free and clear this time, Blanco.'

'No, nothing's certain.'

I tried to stoke the conversation. 'Of course it is. A doddle. Mere formality.' Barrowclough had eased away a little. I felt it would do no harm to draw him back into the chin-wag. I raised my voice a little. 'Even Mr Barrowclough would bet on that, and you know how middle of the road he is on every flaming issue. If you ask him for a straight yes or no, he'll say : "It depends what you mean by yes or no".'

It worked. Barrowclough perked up his ears. 'What was that, Fletcher?'

'I was saying, sir, you are unwilling to commit yourself on issues. Like to hedge your bets, sit on the fence, know what I mean?'

'I do not. I'm as positive in my opinions as the next man.'

'Oh, well then, you'd agree Old Blanco's release is a formality this time round?'

'Oh – well, I'm not sure. I mean, one has to consider both sides.'

I sighed and shook my head. 'Come off it. It's a disgrace he ain't been free and clear years before now.' Then I gave it to Blanco direct. 'You're on your way, pop. Even genial Harry Grout's giving odds on.'

But Blanco didn't seem overchuffed. He sighed. 'I won't bank on nowt, Fletch. Too accustomed to disappointment.'

He glanced thoughtfully down at the board. I said hastily, 'You know your trouble, Blanco? Always insisting you was innocent.'

'What d'you mean by that, Fletch?' Lennie asked.

'I mean, it's the wrong attitude.'

Barrowclough looked puzzled, something he's good at. 'Wrong attitude?' he asked.

'Look, the Parole Board's like everything else inside. You have to play the game the right way. And that means playing the game their way.'

Barrowclough smiled craftily. 'If you're such an expert on how to play the game, how come *you've* never impressed the Board?'

'Because they wants excuses. And I ain't got none. And when Blanco insists on his innocence, he makes the same mistake. You see, for them, it's better to be guilty and ashamed than innocent and defiant.'

Blanco nodded agreement. 'That's true. You have to show them how you've reformed.'

'Right. In other words, you have to prove you've changed. That you ain't as despicable as what you once was. That's why parole's a piece of cake if you once was an alcoholic or a junkie, or dressed up in women's clothes.'

Lennie asked eagerly, 'So what about a bloke like me who only had the occasional lapse into petty crime? Who otherwise came from a decent home and had an O level in Geography? What are my chances?'

'Lock up!' called Mr Barrowclough.

Later that night, as we were waiting in our bunks for lights out, Lennie returned to the subject.

'Fletch?'

'Yeah?'

'You do figure Blanco's a cert, do you? This time?'

'Need the beds, don't they?'

'What was he originally sent up for?'

I gave a reproving "tsk". 'Now, son, you been inside long enough to know you don't ask that. Take people for what they are, not what they was.'

'I know that, Fletch, but come on. Nothing you could say about Blanco would put me off the old boy. He's one of the nicest people in here. He's kind and gentle and helpful. Don't make no difference to me what he's done.'

'He done his wife.'

As I'd expected, this produced a gasp from the bunk below. 'What?'

'Done her in. Locked her in a deep freeze.'

'And we knock around with a bloodthirsty old scroat like that?'

'What did I tell you? You shouldn't ask.'

'I'm sorry. I admit that was an irrational outburst. Any road – long time ago, wasn't it?'

'So it's okay to refrigerate your old lady as long as it's way back in 1959?'

Lennie struggled to find a way out. 'I mean, he's obviously changed. Had time to repent, like.'

'That's just the point : he's never repented. He always claims he never done it. Says it was her lover.'

'What happened to the lover?'

'They could never find him to ask. He disappeared very smartish – so very probably it *was* him.'

Lennie sighed. 'I suppose there's no way of ever knowing now. It happened so long ago.'

'Right. And a wife can't testify against her old man so there's no point turning to the wonders of modern science.'

Lennie asked in a puzzled voice, 'I don't get you, Fletch.'

'No point in defrosting her and asking what really happened.'

Just then the lights went out, leaving us in eerie gloom. 'Pleasant dreams,' I called cheerfully.

The question of Blanco's chances with the Parole Board was not only being discussed by his fellow prisoners. I learned this when I was mopping the landing outside Mr MacKay's office the next day. Inside were MacKay himself and Mr Barrowclough.

'Sixteen new admissions,' the former gasped. 'Where on earth are we going to put them all, Mr Barrowclough?'

'The Parole Board's here tomorrow. So we'll be saying goodbye to some of our better-behaved inmates.'

MacKay laughed. He always manages to make it sound like a threat. 'That's true. Win a few, lose a few. Well, with the board coming, we'd better make a bit of an effort.'

'Shall I tell the kitchen tinned peaches, then?'

'Yes. And ideal milk, I suppose.'

'Very well. What's your estimate on the releases we might expect?'

'I should think we could count on eight at least.'

'They weren't that lenient last time.'

'If you recall, Barrowclough, the last Parole Board had a woman on it. And she wasn't very receptive to most of the men's pleas.'

'Oh yes, Miss Turnbull. An embittered old battle-axe, wasn't she?'

'She was in a bad mood. Coming into the prison, a work party went by, made certain lewd remarks and jostled her.'

'You'd have thought it would have cheered her up. A woman like that can't get jostled too often.'

'Eight releases will still leave me eight beds to find.'

Barrowclough coughed discreetly. 'I've heard our prison bookie is more optimistic. He's offering odds on ten.'

'Is he now?'

'He's very reliable, Grout, isn't he? He picked all six winners in the boxing bouts.'

MacKay snorted. 'Hardly surprising, Barrowclough. He fixed them in the first place.'

Barrowclough sighed deeply and then asked: 'How does he get away with these things, Mr MacKay? Arranging, fixing, manipulating. I mean, what method can he use on his fellow prisoners?'

The evil laugh sounded again. 'It's called terror, Mr Barrowclough.' I could picture the timid Barrowclough shuddering. 'By the way, which parolee has the shortest odds?'

'Well, my favourite's old Blanco Webb.'

'Oh yes, Blanco.'

'Frankly, I was surprised he didn't make it last time.'

'He was one of Miss Turnbull's victims.'

'Really? How did he manage to upset her?'

'She asked him: after seventeen years, what's the first thing you're going to do when you get out – and he told her. Hell, it's time for inspection.'

And MacKay came charging out of his office.

The next day I was relaxing after lunch in the spacious and well-equipped association area when Lennie breezed up. 'Know summat you don't for once,' he chortled.

'That'll be the day.'

'Well, for starters, I know thirteen across.'

I irritably covered the crossword puzzle with my hand. That is one of the many troubles with the nick. There is nothing – but nothing – you can keep to yourself. I rebuked young Godber.

'Do you mind? Height of bad manners, that is.'

'The word is rook. Type of bird, R, two blanks, K. It's got to be rook.'

This jaunty confidence irritated me, specially since I'd been brooding about the word for ten minutes. 'Not necessarily.'

'Fletch! R, two blanks and a K. What else could it be but – rook?'

'What else? Well, just one example, it could be –er – rilk.'

'Rilk?'

'Exactly. Rilk.'

'There's no such bird.'

'That is just where you are wrong, young Godber. You're not quite as smart as you think you are.'

'What's a flaming rilk, then?'

'A very fascinating creature. Your rilk is, as it happens, a migratory bird from the Baltic shores of Northern Finland. Its most distinguishable feature is that it flies backwards to keep the snow out of its eyes. Ask me another, Magnus.'

'It's still rook.'

I sighed and turned the paper over for future use. 'All right, so what's this piece of knowledge you're aching to tell me?'

Lennie sat down beside me.

'First Parole Board results are through.'

'Oh yes?'

'They've turned down Gibson, who's in for car theft, and okayed Mal Brown who's in for manslaughter. I mean, that's barmy, isn't it?'

'Not really. I should say it was an accurate reflection of society's current sense of values.'

'Yes, but – '

'Think of it this way. It takes one minute to create a

life but ten to make a car. And about five minutes for it to fall to pieces. Hey up, Nat Mills and Bobbie.'

This last remark was prompted by the spectacle of old Blanco and Lukewarm ambling towards us.

'Well, the old devil did it this time,' said Lukewarm.

I asked : 'What, worked his parole?'

'He did that. It was that clean shirt.'

I felt a quick pang. Always takes you like that in the nick. You hear someone else is going out and, just for a moment, you want to break his leg. Even if he's a mate, the thought that he's on his way to freedom brings out some buried demon. Still, if anyone deserved it, old Blanco did. After *seventeen years*! I pulled myself together and winked at him.

'Told you, didn't I? Doddle.'

'Be a few changes, though. Since 1959,' Lennie remarked.

'I flogged a hot car in 1959,' I reminisced. 'Ford Zodiac it was. Two-tone with wing mirrors. Took the wife to Butlins on the proceeds. We won a bronze medal in the Tea for Two cha-cha.'

Lennie contributed :

'I were in Junior School in 1959. Sitting next to Ann Podmore. She was left-handed.'

'Bet you got on the right side of her, then.'

Blanco said glumly, 'I remember 1959 only as the year I were sent away for something I didn't do.'

I remonstrated with him. 'Here, listen mate, you're casting a gloom on the proceedings. I mean, we're only trying to be festive.'

Blanco nodded but he looked far from festive. Curiosity, which I'd suppressed for years, got the better of me. I leaned towards Blanco and asked : 'Here, Blanco, now you've swung it, you can level with your mates. Was you innocent all this time?'

Blanco became animated. He said fiercely: 'I was that! Listen, Fletch, I know you'd like to think I've been screwing the system all this time. But the truth is that the system's screwed me for seventeen years. That's why I've come to a decision.'

'Decision?'

'Aye. For all these years, I've stood me ground. I've proclaimed me innocence. If I accept parole now, you know what I'd be doing? I'd be admitting me guilt.'

Naturally, I tried to deflect this unhealthy line of thought. 'Blanco, parole wipes the slate clean. It says you're free and clear.'

'But it's not a pardon. Parole says we'll let you out now and don't be a bad lad again. Well, I were never the bad lad they said I were in the first place. So they can take their parole – and shove it!' With which, Blanco turned smartly and tottered away.

Well, the next chance I had for a bit of a natter with him was the following day. He was working on his pathetic allotment, raking at the patch of stony dust.

'You haven't, have you?' I asked.

He stopped raking. 'I have.'

'Told 'em to stuff it?'

'Aye.'

'What did Governor say, then?'

'Put the wind up his clappers, I know that.'

I sighed at this barmy behaviour. 'You could be on the streets now, you know. Queuing up at the labour exchange. Standing in the rain waiting for a bus.'

'I waited long enough. Bit longer won't make no difference. Can you pass me the watering can?'

I gave it to him and he sprinkled a few drops on to some feeble green stalks. I said encouragingly: 'Rhubarb's coming on a treat.'

'Can't wait to get your hands on my rhubarb, can you?

126

Thought I'd bequeath it to you if I got out, did you? In lieu of Monopoly debts?'

'Don't be daft, Blanco.'

'Perhaps you had your eye on me radishes as well? But I'm still here. And this is still my allotment.'

Could it be? I'd heard of cons who go stir crazy and afraid to face the outside world. Was Blanco refusing parole so he wouldn't be parted from his miserable allotment? I said soothingly: 'We'd have looked after it. You know that, Blanco. Till you came back inside.'

His shoulders drooped and he nodded. 'I reckon you would.' He gazed about at the forlorn patch. 'Just like life, prison. You make plans and do sod all about it. Look at this place. I were going to do so much. Caulies, I thought. And spring onions and big ripe runner beans. Maybe even raspberries and goosegogs . . . Never got round to it. In all that time.'

'Didn't one Governor once let you grow grapes?'

His eyes brightened. 'Aye. I read all about vines. I knew I could grow grapes, even in a place like this. And I did too. Bloody marvel, it were. Seeing those ripe, juicy beauties – and then they made me pack it in.'

'Why?'

'Make wine from grapes, don't they?'

'Do they? Always used potato peelings myself.'

Blanco chuckled at old memories. 'They didn't tumble till we'd got about a dozen bottles put down.'

'Nice drop, was it?'

'In the wine stakes, Fletch, I don't suppose it were a classic. But to a man who hadn't had a drink for eleven years – well, Chateau Slade were the finest drop I ever supped.'

'If you weren't such a stubborn old mule, you could be supping champagne now. Out there.'

'Got me pride.'

'Freedom's pride.'

'Want both, Fletch.'

I nodded. 'Right then – we'll have to see what we can do.'

Saturday afternoon, Barrowclough mooched into the association area and found us doing it. He blinked.

'Saturday, and you're all indoors?'

'Crow,' I explained.

'I beg your pardon?'

'These are the central headquarters of our campaign. C.R.O.W.'

Barrowclough looked hard at the sheets of paper in front of me. He asked : 'And just what would that be?'

'The Committee for the Release of Old Webb. You know – Blanco. We wanted to make it the Committee for the Release and Pardon of Old Webb, but that would have spelled Crapow – which sounds a bit rude when you're petitioning the Home Office.'

'The Home Office?' An apprehensive shiver passed across Barrowclough's bovine features.

'Well, eventually. The Governor first.'

Lennie took up the tale. 'See, old Blanco doesn't want to go out free and guilty. So we have to make sure he goes out free and innocent.'

'Which is what Crow is all about,' croaked Lukewarm.

'Already got three hundred signatures,' Lennie said proudly.

'But what are you petitioning for?'

I enlightened him.

'There's two ways it can be done. One, the Governor has the right to request a pardon from the Home Office, under Sub-section twenty-three, part three, paragraph D, Penal Code as amended by the Act of 1972.'

Barrowclough pawed nervously at the ground. 'Really?'

'Oh yes. Well known, that is.'

'And the other alternative?'

'Demand a retrial.'

'After all this time? I should think the judge, the jury and the witnesses are nearly all deceased by now.'

'Yeah, well, that may be to the old boy's advantage, know what I mean?'

Warren blew in waving a sheet of paper. 'Here, look at this, Fletch. I've done the laundry and machine-shop since yesterday and got sixty-three signatures.'

'Very good, my son.'

But Barrowclough perceived an objection.

'Just a minute. There's no more than forty people at the most working in those two places.'

'Just goes to show the strength of their feelings, don't it?' I pointed out.

Lennie, who had been inspecting the sheet Warren had handed him, murmured : 'Lot of X's on this sheet.'

Bunny shrugged. 'Lot of folk in this nick can't write.'

'How can you be sure that these X's are the genuine article?' Barrowclough demanded.

I took the paper from Godber and held it under Barrowclough's nose. 'Stands to reason, Mr Barrowclough. Look at the difference in the handwriting. See, one bloke's spelled X with a Y.'

Barrowclough. 'Well, I have to admit it's a praiseworthy effort. My only fear is the Governor's attitude. He has an automatic resistance to any notion proposed by you lot.'

'Well, that's just where you could help us, Mr Barrowclough. Add some weight to our pitch, like.'

'How?'

'We know you for a humanitarian. You're no hardnose. You've always played fair with us. Seen our point of view. Your example has brought reason and compassion into a world where too often only violence prevails.'

Barrowclough was visibly swelling under this treatment, like a cow that's been at wet clover. He cleared his throat. 'Well, as you know, I consider you men are here to be helped, not punished. I try to understand, not condemn. I respect your rights and if you have a just cause, I'll back it to the hilt.'

There was a discreet murmur of 'hear-hears' from some of the boys. I said solemnly :

'Never doubted it, sir. So would you just add your monicker here?'

Barrowclough shied faintly. 'Well now – hold on –'

I thrust a pen into his hand. 'Just cause, sir.'

But Barrowclough was shaking his head firmly. 'Oh no, you don't. No ruddy fear. I'm up for promotion next month. I'm not jeopardising that by being party to a prisoners' conspiracy.'

And he turned on his heel and strode away.

Lennie said sadly : 'Not quite the humanitarian we reckoned.'

'No, but give him his due,' I said cheerfully. 'He's smarter than we thought.'

'Pity, though. Get his signature and a few more screws might have followed.'

'So that's what we'll have to do, isn't it?'

'Eh?'

'No sweat.'

I took the pen and bent over the sheet. I wrote very carefully. Warren gaped in admiration.

'Can you really forge Barra's signature, Fletch?'

'How do you think we got the new requisition of ping-pong balls last week?'

Lennie was dubious. He pointed out : 'You'll be for it if they trace it back to you, Fletch.'

'More likely to trace it back to you. It's your pen.'

'What?' Lennie seized it and examined it while I chuckled quietly.

It's amazing. When I have to enter the Governor's office in the line of duty, he's never what you might call frantically busy. Usually he's either chatting up his secretary or gazing moodily out of the window as if yearning for freedom. But any time *I* want to see him he immediately gets plunged into activity. We'd been waiting in his outer office with our petition for what seemed the best part of a month. I'd gone into a kind of trance when Barrowclough suddenly snapped :

'Stop whistling, Fletcher.'

'Eh?'

'I said stop whistling.'

I hadn't even realised that I'd lapsed into melody. I sighed. 'Oh, sorry. Against regulations, is it? "Thou shalt not whistle in the Governor's outer office." New one on me.'

Barrowclough turned on Lennie. 'What do you think you're doing, Godber?'

It was obvious what he was doing. He was whiling away the long winter making paper aeroplanes. On Barrowclough's harsh query, he started guiltily.

'Nothing, Mr Barrowclough.'

He unfolded the plane and replaced it in the in-tray on Mrs Jamieson's desk. I remarked : 'Wish he'd hurry up. I've got a busy day ahead.'

Barrowclough said : 'We've all got a busy day ahead, Fletcher. Difficult period this, just after the Parole Board's been.'

'That's true. All the turn-downs get disappointed and bitter. Breeds hostility. Even violence.'

'Yes, it's quite unlike the week before the board get here. You're all on your best behaviour then. Butter wouldn't melt.'

'That's right. Even Mad Dog Hollister didn't hit any-one last week.'

Lennie grinned. 'He's hit a few since they turned him down. And set fire to his mattress. And assaulted the Chaplain.'

Just then MacKay sprang out of the inner office like some hideous clockwork figure. He barked: 'All right, Mr Barrowclough, wheel them in.'

Since they had neglected to kit us out with wheels, Barrowclough had to content himself with marching us in. Once inside, we stood firmly to attention in front of the Governor's desk while Venables pretended to be engrossed in the study of what I could, by using my amazing talent for reading upside-down, see was an old shopping list. Finally he glanced up. Barrowclough said simply :

'Crow, sir.'

'What? Why?'

'Er – no, sir – Crow. You remember? The Committee for the Release of Old Webb, sir. Blanco, sir. I men-tioned it to you, sir – the petition.'

Venables snorted. 'Oh, that, yes. I'm not in favour of prisoners' pressure groups.'

Barrowclough, with a miserable lack of tact, just barged on. 'They have the right, Governor, under sub-section thirteen which clearly states that in the event of – '

Venables held up a peevish hand. 'Don't spout the penal code at me, Barrowclough.'

Since it was clear that Barrowclough was going to be about as subtle as a stampeding long-horn, I said quickly : 'Let us say straight off, Governor, sir, how much we appreciate you seeing us. May I present, sir, for your perusal and consideration this petition for the retrial of Old Man Blanco, sir.'

Venables sighed but accepted the sheets I held out to him. He perused them languidly. Finally, he asked : 'Do we have this many men here?'

Lennie said ingratiatingly : 'The petition, sir, is a sincere expression of the feeling in Slade Prison. And the fact that they have responded in this way is a tribute to your enlightened administration.'

This was heady stuff. Venables blinked. 'Is it?'

I pressed our advantage. 'Oh, most certainly, sir. All them blokes out there, burly felons, putting their names to a piece of paper. In, as the lad puts it, a less enlightened administration, they'd have torn the place apart by now.'

An outraged growl issued from MacKay. 'Is that a threat, Fletcher?'

'Not a threat, sir, no. Just an observation. Based on several years of first-hand experience of the mood of the incarcerated male.'

Venables tapped the petition. 'The mood is really as strong as this?' I nodded. 'Growing stronger ever minute, sir – and uglier. Present company excepted, of course.'

MacKay appealed to the Governor. 'What is the point of this, sir? The authorities have been compassionate enough to offer Webb parole. He should accept it and be grateful.'

I said humbly, 'It's just not enough, Mr MacKay. He has to clear his name, see?'

MacKay snorted. 'The man's an old fool.'

Barrowclough rallied briefly to the cause. 'No, I wouldn't say that. Stubborn, but not foolish. In fact, there's something quite heroic – er – quite – well – something – er – as you say, the man's a fool.'

His sudden indecision has been caused by an encounter with one of MacKay's most corrosive glares. His voice trailed away into silence. Venables turned to me.

'You must remember, Fletcher, that Webb was found guilty by a jury of his peers.'

This was my big scene. I gave it all I had. 'Sir, we know he's innocent. Me and all the lads. I mean, we're all cons, ain't we? We knows when one of our own is spinning the yarn. You lot mightn't, but we do.'

'The case was too long ago, Fletcher, for a retrial.'

'Ah, but there's ways and means, sir. This petition's only the first step in making this a national issue.'

Venables drew in his breath sharply. 'National?'

Lennie dished out the next instalment. 'We want to make old Blanco a national hero, sir. We want to touch the conscience of the nation. We want the spotlight of the mass media on the old fellow.'

Venables actually paled. 'Mass media?'

I came in on cue : 'That's it, Governor, create a folk hero through the television and the newspapers. Why, you'll be a celebrity yourself, sir. Might even get on the Parkinson show. Esther Rantzen's a cert.'

But MacKay said firmly : 'There's no way that this petition could escalate into a national issue.'

I'd been waiting for this. 'You're absolutely right, Mr MacKay. As things stand, there's no way. That's why we need the hunger strike.'

Venables clutched the edge of his desk. 'What hunger strike?'

I said sympathetically, 'Old Blanco's. It would be an ordeal for us all, sir. But don't worry, it couldn't last long. I mean, a man his age shouldn't go more than a week top weight.'

What's called a pregnant silence fell upon the company. MacKay glared. Barrowclough shuffled. Lennie and I gazed upwards as if at the celestial reward that would, if nothing else, be Blanco's at the end of his hunger strike. Venables rallied first. He tapped the petition and, with a faint gulp, said : 'All right, you can leave this here. Now — back to your cells.'

I said quickly, 'Can we return, sir, in the knowledge that you're giving the matter your due consideration?'

But MacKay barked : 'Fletcher! On your way.'

And out we marched.

What happened after we'd gone, as Barrowclough admitted later, was that consternation reigned. The Governor, as anticipated, did not relish presiding over the slow demise of a nice old con who might even be innocent. But what could he do? What? It was then that Barrowclough remembered an obscure sub-section in the penal code, because I'd made sure he would by mentioning it about five times a day for the past week.

'There might be a solution to this problem, sir,' he had said to the Governor. 'I'm sure you're aware of it, given your knowledge of the penal code.'

'Er – refresh my memory, Mr Barrowclough.'

'Sub-section 23, part 3, paragraph D.'

'Ah yes . . . Yes, good old sub-section 23, paragraph G.'

'D, sir, paragraph D.'

'D, yes. Of course. Er, jog my memory again, will you, Mr Barrowclough.'

'Well, as you know, sir, under special circumstances the Governor of a prison has the right, if his discretion feels it's warranted – '

'Yes,' the Governor said quickly.

'To request the Home Office for a prisoner's pardon.'

'A pardon?'

'That's right, sir.'

'It would certainly put paid to the news of a hunger strike being splashed across the newspapers.'

'Well, all round, by and large, it does seem a good idea,' Barrowclough finished lamely.

'Yes, well, I'm paid to come up with ideas in situations

like this. I'll submit a recommendation to the Home Office. Can we get rid of those?' He started to hand the petition to MacKay, when something caught his eye. 'Just a minute. Your signature's on this, Mr Barrowclough.'

'Oh no, sir,' said Barrowclough, looking for his spectacles. 'Some mistake, sir.'

MacKay pointed at the signature. 'Look, man,' he barked. 'Is that not your signature?'

'It must be a forgery.' Barrowclough looked at it. 'No, that's definitely my signature. I must have signed it.'

So that was why Lukewarm was able to amble into our flowery some days later and announce : 'Gentlemen, may I present the best-dressed man of 1959.'

He was closely followed by a vision to delight any nostalgia freak's heart : Blanco clad in a seventeen-year-old grey suit. I nodded approvingly.

'Oh yes. Very elegant. Where d'you nick that, Blanco? Burton's?'

He answered shyly, 'I think it were Fifty Shilling Tailors, January sale.'

'They're back in fashion,' Lennie enthused.

'I think in fifty-nine,' I reminisced, 'I wore Italian pinstripes and a shirt with a Billy Eckstein collar.'

Lennie admitted. 'I wore grey flannel shorts.'

Lukewarm glanced down at his faded prison denims and sighed : 'I think I wore much the same as I do now.'

'I wore this suit to wife's funeral,' Blanco said.

I was a little shocked. 'Hardly black, is it?'

'Couldn't afford another suit. Only just finishing paying for that damn freezer. Terrible to think she finished up inside it. Mind you, I suppose it were fitting in a way, because all her life she were a cold woman.'

Barrowclough poked his head in.

'Don't be long, Mr Webb. Bus is waiting.'

He withdrew his bonce. Blanco smiled. 'By gum, do you know how good that sounds? *Mister* Webb.'

'When you goes out there, hold your head up high, my son,' I said.

'I will that, Fletch.' The old lag paused and when he next spoke there was a catch in his voice. 'I'm not very good, you know, after all this time like, at expressing gratitude. But I know what you done – and I'll not forget.'

The catch proved catching and I gulped before saying breezily : 'You're away, pops. All that matters.'

Lennie helped out by observing, 'You've got a lot of living to make up for. Don't waste your time nattering with the likes of us.'

Blanco shook his head. 'I don't want much from life.'

'I know,' I said, 'but it's good that justice has been done – albeit a little late. This pardon's for your family name, for your children and your grandchildren. That's why we done it. So's you can walk out of here and look any man in the face without shame or guilt. Life's taken a lot from you, me old mate, but all you need back from it is your pride, right?'

'Right, Fletch.'

'And naturally there's one more thing.'

'What's that, Fletch?'

'You sue the Government for every bleeding penny you can get.'

Blanco said stoutly, 'Too bloody true, I will.'

Lukewarm seized Blanco's hand and said touchingly : 'You always were a cantankerous, stubborn old mule – but I'll miss you.'

Blanco smiled. 'Thanks. I'll try and get that scented notepaper that you want.'

Just then a terrible thought struck me. It was based on knowledge of Blanco's fierce sense of justice. I grabbed him by the arm.

'Here, listen, Blanco. We knows you didn't do in your old lady and that means some other bloke did. Now you've been incarcerated here for seventeen years for a murder you didn't commit. It wouldn't be natural if you hadn't often thought of taking vengeance on the real culprit. But don't do it, my old son, don't do it!'

Blanco sighed. 'I know who did it, Fletch. It were the wife's lover. But I can promise you I won't touch him.'

'How can you be sure, Blanco?'

'Because he's dead.'

'You know that for a fact?'

'Webb!' came the evil bellow of MacKay, for the last time as far as Blanco was concerned. 'Let's be having you.'

Blanco edged towards the door. I said urgently: 'Blanco, do you know for a fact that he's dead?'

He nodded and said simply: 'That I do know, Fletch. I killed him. Cheerio.'

And the old man tottered off to freedom.

A Test of Character

Who won the Battle of Hastings? I bleeding didn't. What happened in 1253? A lot of poor sods were locked up. How do I know? Because that's what happens every year. And always has done. So what use is History? Very little. The only time I thought it might have some value was when me, Charley Ambrose and two other lads hijacked a lorry full of Bacardi rum which turned out, because of a mess-up, to contain about a million history textbooks. But we couldn't find a fence that would even look at them. In the end we dumped them in the River Ouse, where they fouled up the intake of a power station and plunged Goole into darkness. So much for the light of learning. Which was the lesson I'd been trying to drive home to Lennie ever since he'd started his new studies. I mean a dell is not the British Museum, is it?

'Naff off, Fletch!' he urged irritably.

I gazed at him in resentment. A moment before I had been feeling positively chuffed. I had thrashed Warren, McLaren and a timid poofter from D Block called Wiggins in quick succession at draughts. Three quarters of an ounce of good shag in my pocket testified to my triumph. Is it any wonder that I was carolling a cheerful song as I entered our little domain? And what did I get?

'Naff off, Fletch!'

'I beg your pardon, Godber?'

He didn't even glance up from his array of books. But he stopped sucking the end of his pencil long enough to say: 'You heard.'

I sighed and shook my head. 'Shall I tell you something, Godber? Prison's coarsened you, my lad.'

He kept his eyes down but was gracious enough to remark : 'Yeah. Well, it's hardly finishing school, is it?'

'Nevertheless, when you first come in here, you did retain some vestiges of old-world courtesy – such as respect for your elders.'

'When I first come in here, *you* taught me the value of peace and quiet. I'm in agreement with that now.'

'Meaning?'

'Meaning : do not disturb. I'm trying to study.'

This passion for learning was doing nothing for our relationship. It was like sharing a cell with a waxwork, except that a waxwork would not have kept grumbling at the slightest sound. But my motto is and always has been live and let live.

'Very well,' I conceded. 'Not another word.'

'Thanks, Fletch,' he acknowledged, and then muttered some dates under his breath.

I wanted him to feel completely reassured, so I added : 'Not a single, solitary word will emit from my lips forthwith – forthwith my lips are sealed. Yes, sealed are forthwith my lips. I have sealed forth my lips with – '

'Fletch !' he cried in exasperation.

'What?'

'You weren't going to say nowt.'

'And I'm not. Honest. Not a peep. Schtum. With a capital Scht.'

He gave me a doubtful look and returned to his studies. I was about to heave myself on to my bunk when I thought of a good one. Even thinking about it made me chuckle inwardly. The lad would fall about. So I approached him and said : 'Here, Len – '

He jumped and exclaimed : 'Oh, naffin' heck !'

I hastened to reassure him. 'No, no, this won't take a minute.'

'Well, what is it?'

I cupped my hands and held them out to him. 'Guess what I've got in here?' I asked, keeping a straight face.

He didn't seem exactly on fire with curiosity. 'I don't care, Fletch. Go away, would you, please?'

'No, it's a good one this. Have a guess. What have I got in my hands? Go on then.'

He sighed deeply. Still running his eyes along the page, he grunted, 'Okay. A cockroach.'

'No.'

'I give up,' he said unsportingly.

But I wasn't having that. 'You got two more guesses.'

'A walnut.'

'A walnut?' I exclaimed. 'Why should I have a bleeding walnut?'

'All right,' said Lennie, with an air of finality. 'It's a naffing giraffe with a hare lip wearing purple Y-fronts.'

I could not forbear a reproachful look. Height of bad manners, that is, knowing the end of a joke and not letting on.

'Who told you?' I asked sullenly.

'Fletch, naff off!' he exclaimed, a touch of real anger in his voice. 'I've asked you nicely. I have an exam and I need to study.'

'Okay,' I conceded. 'I have no objection to your studying. But this is not the most suitable place for it.'

'Where do you suggest?'

'Well, the education room would seem to fit the bill. Yes, I think that would be most appropriate.'

'Except that there's a lecture in there tonight. The Accident Prevention Officer is speaking on industrial safety.'

'That's been cancelled,' I said haughtily.

'Has it?'

'Yeah. On his way here the Accident Prevention

Officer fell off his bike. He's in Carlisle General now.'

'I wish you were,' Lennie murmured.

'I see,' I said reproachfully. 'Well, just remember there are two people to a cell, Godber. And it's very unsettling for a social misfit like me to have someone sat here who wants to better himself.'

He swung round at this and his eyes blazed. Never seen the lad in such a temper before. 'Yeah? Well, when I get out of here, I may have another "O" Level. What will you have to show for it? Just another stretch done !'

'Is that so?' I asked, with scathing irony. I was trying to think of a follow-up that blended dignity with truth when MacKay bounded into the dell like a jackal.

'Oh yes, oh yes,' he snarled.

'Ah, the town crier,' I exclaimed.

'What's going on here? A heated exchange, is it? Raised voices?'

I was not sorry for the distraction.

'Oh, here it is,' I announced. 'Mother superior.'

'Watch your lip, Fletcher.'

'My lips are sealed, sir. Forthwith my lips are sealed.'

Lennie muttered : 'If only that were true.'

MacKay, adopting his hypocritical fatherly tone, asked the lad : 'What's the problem, Godber?'

But, of course, Lennie was not going to grass, angry though he was. 'Nothing, Mr MacKay.'

'Fletcher getting on your wick?' the screw prompted. 'No, sir.'

'Trying to study, are we? I'm afraid that won't cut much ice with an ageing recidivist like Fletcher.'

Lennie looked up. 'Ageing what?'

'Recidivist,' repeated MacKay smugly. 'A person who pays his penance for performing a crime, goes out and straight off performs another one.'

'He means,' I pointed out sardonically, 'a professional.'

'No,' thundered MacKay, turning to me, 'I mean an habitual criminal. Something which you might have avoided, Fletcher, if you'd got stuck into your education like laddo here.'

I shrugged.

'Yeah, well, I never finished school, did I?'

Lennie sighed and abandoned his studies.

'How come?' he asked.

'War, wasn't it? Always playing truant. Out with the lads, on the bomb sites, collecting shrapnel and that. Learning about sex in air-raid shelters during their off-peak hours. So eventually they sent me to a special school with other kids what was always playing truant. But we never learned nothing.'

'And why not?' asked MacKay.

'No one ever showed up for school.'

MacKay smiled complacently. His chest began to swell as he boasted : 'See me, I had to leave school at fourteen. Help bring a living wage into the house. Hard times in those days in the Lanarkshire coalfields. My father was an unemployed miner with eight children to provide for.'

'Eight kids, eh? He wasn't unemployed the whole time, then?' I commented.

'Let me tell you something, Fletcher, not one of our family neglected education. Even under the most difficult circumstances, like those of Godber here. I've had to pass exams, you know. You don't get to be a warrant officer in the Army without something up here.' At this point the nurk patted the thistle he used for a head. 'As well as something in there.' And he thumped his puffed-out chest.

'And kissing somewhere else?' I queried.

His eyes narrowed to slits. 'Did I hear you correctly, Fletcher?'

'No, you didn't, sir,' I hastily amended.

He contented himself with a fierce glare. Then he shook his thistle. 'You're a lost cause, Fletcher.' He turned back to the lad. 'What subject are you studying, Godber?'

'History, sir. O level like. Already got one O level before I come inside. Geography.'

I exclaimed : 'Gawd, you're so proud of your geography. It ain't got no application in real life, you know? Ain't going to do you no good knowing what an escarpment is. Or what's the capital of Finland.'

'Helsinki,' supplied Lennie promptly.

'Hell's teeth !' I groaned.

MacKay frowned. 'Get out of here, Fletcher,' he ordered.

I looked at him in amazement. 'What?'

'Go on – make yourself scarce.'

This was blatant harassment. I protested : 'I just come in from work. I'm entitled – '

'You're entitled to nothing in here except to obey the sound of my voice.'

I nodded. 'Right,' I said grimly. 'I see. How long am I supposed to absent myself for then?'

'Until lock up.'

I shrugged. 'I'll make it later if you like. Give us the keys and I'll let myself in.'

MacKay took a threatening step towards me. 'Out !' he snapped.

I turned with quiet dignity and strolled out of the dell.

Now in Muswell Hill, if I'd had a tiff with my nearest and dearest, I should just have continued strolling with quiet dignity until I'd reached the saloon bar of The Dragoon. Once there, six or eight pints and the sympathetic ears of a few mates would have rapidly healed the wound. But the architect of Slade Nick had inexcusably neglected to include a bar. So all I could do was take my load of grief to the association area, where all I beheld was a gang of dishonest felons indulging themselves in trivial pastimes.

'Evening,' I remarked, as pleasantly as I could.

Manners in the nick compare unfavourably with those of the average barnyard. No one even glanced up. Since there was practically no room on any of the benches, I asked courteously: 'Is it too much trouble to ask you gentlemen to budge up and give me a seat?'

Oaths and grumbling greeted this civil request. But a slight shifting of criminal bottoms followed. I planted myself on the edge of the plank. I glanced about moodily. That's another difference from your cheery local. In a pub you may chance to make a rewarding new aquaintance. In the nick, every bleeding face is familiar. I spotted Warren and McLaren and Spraggon, who had a paper.

'Spraggs?' I addressed the last-mentioned.

'What?'

'Two's up with that paper, eh?'

'You'll have to wait,' he grunted. 'I'm going to do the crossword.'

'You don't need all the paper just to do the crossword,' I pointed out.

'I do,' he retorted unconvincingly.

I called across to two convicts who were enjoying a game of draughts: 'I'll play the winner.'

'No, I am,' announced Warren rudely.

'I see,' I said. I turned to McLaren. ''Ere, Jock.'

'What?' asked Prester Jock.

I cupped my hands. 'What have I got in my hands then?'

A number of disgruntled voices, in ragged unison, bawled: 'Heard it!'

I sighed deeply. 'That is what I shall miss most when I get out of prison – the bonhomie.'

McLaren growled : 'If you don't like it here, naff off to your pit.'

I shook my head and explained politely : ' 'Fraid I can't do that. Can't stay in me own flowery dell in case it upsets His Nibs' concentration.'

Bunny said emphatically : 'Mean a lot to Godber, that exam.'

'Won't open no doors,' I maintained.

Spraggon looked up from his paper. 'Nowt wrong with education. Doing it meself. Writing a book, I am. Manifesting my literary bent.'

I nodded. 'Oh yes, I heard about your literary aspirations, Spraggs. We're all very relieved to hear that you're laying down the sword and picking up the pen. As are a lot of battered night watchmen round your way.'

'Spraggs is right,' insisted Warren. 'If we'd all had some education we wouldn't be here now.'

I laughed bitterly. 'Don't give me that. Us lot was destined to end up in here. If we'd had education we'd have just been in for a better class of crime. Stock manipulation or fraudulent conversion.'

'I know a lot of knowledge,' Warren announced.

'Don't be daft,' I rebuked him, 'you can't even read.'

'Maybe not,' maintained Bunny, 'but I get it from the telly. Schools programmes, University Challenge, Sale of the Century. I learn things and I digest them with my retentative memory. Shall I give you an example?'

'No,' I grunted.

But Warren is not easily discouraged. 'Right,' he said. 'Apparently – 'ere, listen, Spraggs – if every Chinaman in China jumped up and down – at the same moment, like – it would cause a tidal wave which would engulf America.' He gazed about triumphantly.

Spraggon wrinkled his brow. 'Food for thought,' he pronounced.

An anxious look came into Bunny's face. 'Or is it Australia?' he wondered aloud.

McLaren nodded wisely. 'Either way. Secret weapon there.'

I contributed: 'Be ironical, wouldn't it? President Carter gets the world to agree to ban all nuclear weapons. Then, before the ink's dry on the treaty, the Chinks leap up and down and "whoosh" – world domination.'

Spraggon, having run the matter through the mill of his mighty intellect, shook his head. 'Bit unlikely.'

'Not with them Chinese,' I insisted. 'If anyone could pull it off they could. Because they're regimented. Do everything by numbers. Look at the menu in a Chinese restaurant. But it would never work in England.'

'We could do it if we put our minds to it,' Warren declared patriotically.

'Not a snowball's,' I maintained. 'The British working man would never leap in the air in case he spilt his tea.'

'Still,' boasted Bunny, 'that's knowledge, isn't it?'

'Oh yes. May I enquire where you got this fascinating piece of information?' I asked.

'Someone read it to me once from a magazine in this chiropodist's waiting room,' he offered.

'What was wrong with you, then? Toothache?'

'No, I was there with me feet.'

'Naturally,' I said hopefully.

'I've always had these feet, like,' Warren went on. 'It's a good chiropodist, though. They're very quick.'

'Do they do them while you wait?' I asked.

'Eh?'

'I mean, or do they say leave 'em with us, they'll be ready Thursday. Soled and heeled.'

'Get off, Fletch. You're pulling my leg.'

'I wouldn't dare. Your foot might come off.'

'No, listen,' Bunny said, 'I've got some more knowledge. About planets.'

'Oh Gawd – ' I began, but Warren ploughed on.

'If the sun was here,' he announced, holding up his cupped hands to show the position, 'about the size of a football, and the earth was at the end of the table where Fletch is – '

'Oh dear, have I got any on my trousers?' I asked, but he ignored me.

'Now on that scale – where would the nearest star be?'

Felonious brows wrinkled in deep thought. McLaren asked suspiciously : 'Is this one of them trick questions?'

'No, no,' Warren protested, 'straight up.'

But McLaren wanted his reservations put on record. 'Because if it is I'll stuff you, Warren.'

Spraggon held up a hand for silence. 'Let's see. Sun there and earth there. Nearest star? Long way, I know that – I'd say the recreation yard.'

'Wrong,' exclaimed Bunny happily.

'Not by far, I'll bet,' grumbled the humiliated Spraggon.

'Wait and see,' promised the crafty Warren. 'Jock, what do you say?'

'It's further than that,' pronounced Black Jock. 'Married quarters.'

'Wrong,' crowed Bunny. 'Fletch?'

I sighed dismissively. 'I don't care, do I?'

'No, go on,' wheedled the tiresome scholar, 'have a guess. Like I said, the scale – '

I cut him off. 'Yes, yes, thank you, Magnus Magnusson.'

But McLaren, wanting a companion in humiliation, urged : 'Go on then, Fletcher. You know it all.'

'In a minute,' I agreed, ticking off some numbers on my fingers. 'Just doing the calculations, ain't I? Earth – sun –

allow for the speed of light – carry two – plus the hypotenuse – Carlisle.'

'Wrong!' screamed Bunny, insane with delight.

'Wrong?' I asked stiffly.

'Not even close. You all want to know?'

'Get on with it,' growled McLaren.

Warren gazed about at us like a conjurer with his hand in the top hat. Then he pulled out the rabbit. 'Johannesburg,' he announced.

While we were still gazing at him in disbelief, a furrow crinkled his brow and he added: 'Or is it Australia? Well, either way, it's still fascinating.'

This folly had gone far enough. 'Warren,' I said pointedly, 'I can imagine no possible circumstances where that piece of information would mean naff all to no one. It's like Godber's perishing History. Ain't got no application in real life. Now if it were arithmetic he were doing I could see the point in that. He could work out an up and down treble in his head.'

McLaren nodded. 'He could also work out how long the odds were against him passing.'

'Right,' I agreed.

'Specially,' continued the sooty Scot with a peculiar emphasis, 'sharing a cell with you.'

He was getting at something. But what? 'Pardon?' I asked.

'I said, especially sharing a cell with you.'

'And just what's that supposed to imply?'

McLaren shrugged.

'It's tough enough to study inside. But you – you distract him. And you're always putting him down. You're a destructive influence on the lad.'

'That's true,' agreed Spraggon.

'Hold your bleeding horse,' I protested. 'If Godber passes that exam it will be due in no small part to me.'

'How?' asked Bunny.

'How? I've been tutoring him, ain't I? Up all night sometimes. Learning him about the second world war, as told by someone what lived through it.'

Spraggon smiled craftily. 'All very well, but his subject's the Napoleonic wars.'

I shrugged. 'A war is a war. It's all history, ain't it?'

McLaren exclaimed contemptuously: 'My God, if you've been tutoring him, the odds are even longer than I've imagined. You'd be better off having money on a pit pony in the national.'

I began see what he was getting at.

'All right,' I said, 'let's talk about odds then.'

'You'd bet on him passing?'

'With complete confidence. Name your odds.'

'Evens is good enough for me.'

Sarcasm was called for. 'Oh, the odds have been slashed, haven't they? Moment ago he was a rank outsider.'

'I'm not greedy,' maintained the crafty hybrid. 'Money for old rope this.'

'How much old rope you want to bet then?'

'Ounce of shag.'

To my surprise, and slight alarm, two voices came from the other end of the table:

'I'm on that.'

'Me too.'

Still, honour was at stake. 'Very well then,' I agreed. 'Anyone else?'

'I'm betting on Godber,' proclaimed Bunny loyally. 'If Fletch reckons it.'

'Thank you, Warren,' I said feelingly.

McLaren turned to Spraggon. 'Get on this, Spraggs.'

But the literary bruiser shook his head. 'No thanks. Last bet I had got me in here.'

'How's that?'

'Me and my brother, Malcolm, were casing a ware-house in Fazakerley. And I turned to him and I said : "I bet that Alsatian's no bother".' With which he rose and limped away.

It was not long before pressing business called McLaren away too. That left Bunny and me together.

He asked nervously : 'Have I – er – have I done the right thing, Fletch?'

With more confidence than I felt, I asked : 'Bunny, have I ever let you down?'

'No, Fletch, but it's not easy. Slade Prison has a terrible academic record.'

I pointed out reassuringly : 'Bloke got O level in Spanish last year, didn't he? What was his name? Oh yeah, Gomez.'

Warren looked doubtful but he said bravely, 'Well, you really know Lennie. That's what impressed me, Fletch, your faith in the lad.'

'Yuh, well – I have every faith in him, of course. I know the lad. I know his diligence, his application.'

Warren nodded thoughtfully. We looked at each other. I continued : 'Mind you, while I harbour no doubts as to his ability, he'll have to know the right answers before the exam.'

'How could he, Fletch?'

'We'll have to whip the exam paper.'

In pursuit of this scholarly aim, Bunny and I made our way, at a suitable time, to the Education Room. Alas, it was not unoccupied. This was predictable since it is always locked up when not in use. But what I hadn't bargained for was that a screw would be there. Barrow-clough was in the midst of a little heart-to-heart with Spraggon. The door was ajar and Bunny and I hovered outside, hoping that Barrowclough would depart. He was saying : 'This – er – manuscript of yours, Spraggon. It's very interesting – brutal but interesting.'

'Would mean a lot to me,' pronounced the Dickens of Slade Prison, 'if I became a writer. Nobody in my family's ever been famous, except for me cousin, Ernie.'

'Your cousin Ernie Spraggon was a notorious tearaway,' Barrowclough demurred.

'Famous, though, wasn't he? He made the top ten.'

'Top ten most wanted men, yes.'

'Made a name for himself, though. Couldn't go in a post office without seeing Ernie's photo, could you?'

Barrowclough sighed. 'Look, Spraggon, writing could be your escape, if you'll pardon the expression, and I would be the last one to discourage that. But I think we should start with some grammatical essentials. For example, on page one, the first paragraph, you've left out the 'k' in knuckle duster. And also in kneecaps.'

'Kneecaps?' asked Spraggon, the reference escaping him.

'Yes,' clarified Barrowclough, 'the ones you break with a cricket bat at the top of page two.'

Spraggon burst out in the exasperated tone of the artist who has no time for petty details : 'Look, I know I ain't put much grammar in there. I know my spelling leaves a lot to be desired, like, but I didn't want to interrupt me stream of self-consciousness, did I? See, I write with me gut.'

Barrowclough agreed feelingly. 'I noticed that.'

'All right, so it's brutal, but I'm writing what I know about and I've led a very full and brutal life. I've been warring with the scuffers all me life. Ever since they found me up a Jigger with a fifteen-year-old Judy.'

Barrowclough asked faintly : 'She was only fifteen?'

'I didn't know. I was only twelve meself. I was big for me age, see.'

By this time, it was clear to Bunny and me that this learned discussion might go on indefinitely. We held a hurried conference and put our special emergency plan into operation. First step was to push open the door and barge in. On seeing Barrowclough, I drew back.

'Oh, 'scuse me, Mr Barrowclough.'

He looked up in surprise. The surprise increased when he saw what I was carrying : a football, an orange and a ping-pong ball.

'What is it, Fletcher? What do you men want?'

'We're looking for the Education Officer, sir. The one with the brains, you know.'

'Mr Kingsley's taking a class,' explained the screw. 'I'm just helping him out with some of his more bru – er, basic pupils.'

I nodded sympathetically. 'Well then, Mr Barrowclough, perhaps you'd grant us a moment of your time – in your capacity as a teacher.'

Barrowclough looked suspicious, like a cow contemplating an electric fence. 'You've never shown any interest in education before, Fletcher.'

'Times change, sir,' I assured him. 'Sooner or later a man acquires a thirst for learning. Right, Warren?'

'Right, Fletch. I'm dead thirsty.'

Barrowclough sighed. 'Well, explain what you want briefly. We're busy in here.'

Warren proclaimed : 'We want you to settle an argument.'

'An intellectual argument,' I added.

'Can't it wait?' asked Barrowclough. 'I'm dealing with Spraggon here.'

'Spraggs is used to waiting,' I pointed out. 'Been waiting parole for four years.'

Spraggon took this in good part. 'Be my guest,' he invited.

'Very well then,' nodded Barrowclough. 'What is it?'

I warmed to the task. 'Well, me and the lads was sitting around our cell discussing the wonders of the universe.'

'You were what?' exclaimed the screw incredulously.

'Yeah, this great and wondrous galaxy what still enthrals man with its magnitude and mystery. Anyway, Warren has a theory what I'm disputing.'

'What theory?'

'I'll show you, Mr Barrowclough,' I promised and I flourished the football. 'What I've got here is a scale model of the universe. You see, this football represents the sun.' I placed it carefully on the floor. 'Now this ping-pong ball represents the planet Mercury, and it goes – one, two, three – here.' And I placed it down near the door. 'Give or take a million miles, that is. Now Venus should come next but we'll skip it 'cos we ain't got a prune. Warren threw it out 'cos it was wrinkled. And this orange is the earth, and it goes – ' At this point I gazed about in bewilderment. I couldn't fit the whole solar system into the Education Room. So I said respectfully : 'Could you just step out in the corridor, Mr Barrowclough? Galaxy won't fit in this room, it seems.'

Shaking his head in exasperation, the screw rose and accompanied me, muttering : 'For the life of me, Fletcher, I can't think what you're on about.'

'All in good time, sir.'

I stepped out of the door. Barrowclough turned to Spraggon. 'Will you excuse me for a moment, Spraggon?'

He nodded. 'Yeah, go on like.'

Whereupon Barrowclough and I vacated the dismal hole. As soon as I'd gone, Warren, as he described in detail afterwards, said urgently to the kneecap-buster, 'Hey, Spraggs, where does the Education Officer keep his keys?'

'Keys for what?'

'Filing cabinet through there.'

Spraggon was puzzled. 'Why? There's nowt in there worth lifting. I looked first day in here.'

Bunny glanced anxiously at the door through which Barrowclough and I had departed. Then he pleaded: 'Ask no questions. Please, Spraggs.'

But the burly author smelled a rat. 'Hey, hey, hey,' he protested. 'He's helped me, has Barra. He may be a screw, but he's okay. Before I knew him, I didn't know a semicolon from an apostrophe. When me book's published, I might dedicate it to him because he trusts me, and you're only asking me to betray that trust, right? Well, naff off!'

Warren wasted no further time on emotional appeals. 'Tell us where the keys are and you've made yourself an ounce of snout.'

'In the top drawer,' said Spraggon promptly.

In no more time than it takes to cry 'stop thief!', Warren was at the desk Spraggon had indicated and had the drawer open. At this point he froze with an innocent smile on his face. His reason for doing this was that Mr Barrowclough, in spite of my attempts to restrain him, had re-entered the Education Room. He bore down on Bunny who, thinking he'd been nobbled, was wondering whether to cut and run. But Barrowclough simply pulled open another drawer and drew out two fine red apples.

'There we are,' he said in satisfaction. 'Jupiter and Saturn.' And he joined me again in the corridor.

Warren then completed his mission. He seized the keys, darted into the inner office, unlocked the filing cabinet and withdrew a sealed, official envelope. He placed this under his jacket and returned to the outer office just as Barra and I came in again through the other door. The screw, who was now fully involved in the stars, was saying : 'I know the nearest one is Alpha Centauri. Bit of a hobby of mine, astronomy.'

I glanced at Bunny to find out if he'd secured the goods. He nodded. So I said dismissively to Barrowclough : 'Right then – '

But Barra was gazing abstractedly at the football. He shook his head doubtfully : 'But on this scale – let's see – I wouldn't have thought it was Johannesburg.'

'Yeah, well, thanks, Mr Barrowclough,' I said with finality. 'If you get the right answer, let us know. You know where to find us. Come on, then, Warren. Sorry, Spraggs.'

Bunny and I made a beeline for the door. On the way, I handed him Jupiter. Barrowclough called after us : 'Just a minute, could you return my – '

We turned, each of us taking a large bite of apple. His face fell. 'Oh well – never mind – '

As we left, I heard Barrowclough ask forlornly : 'Do you suppose, Spraggon, that they enacted that whole charade simply to steal my apples?'

Warren and I lost no time in conveying our treasure back to the flowery. There, inevitably, we found Godber bent over his books.

'Still hard at it, are we?' I asked cheerfully.

The lad groaned. 'Trying, yes.'

'Know what they say?' I chided him. 'All work and no play makes Jack a dull beanstalk or something – '

'Do us a favour, Fletch – '

I could not forbear a wink at Bunny. 'Already have, my son.'

He sighed. 'All right, you left the cell for half an hour. Did you have to come back so soon?'

'Knew you'd miss me, little treasure. Knew you'd be worried if I didn't come back before nightfall.'

He put down his pencil. 'Where have you been?'

'Down the Education Room.'

'You?' he asked in amazement. 'What for?'

'Well, we was inspired by your example, wasn't we, Warren?'

'Oh, aye.'

I continued: 'We want to become educated, like what you are.'

Lennie said wearily: 'Do you know, Fletch, one of the main reasons I want to pass this exam tomorrow is so's I have a chance of *not* ending up like you.'

I frowned. 'I'll have to think about that a minute. It's an insult, isn't it?'

Warren tsk-tsked. 'Ungrateful, that's what. If he only knew.'

Lennie, who had once more applied himself to learning, asked with scant interest: 'Knew what?'

'Knew how much Fletch cares,' elaborated Bunny.

'No, no,' I exclaimed, trying to keep the hurt from me voice, 'don't bother him.'

'Cares about what?' asked Lennie.

'Cares about you,' insisted Warren. 'That's what.'

With a catch in my throat, I murmured: 'One day perhaps – '

'No, go on, tell him, Fletch,' urged Warren. 'Tell his nibs what you just done for his benefit at great personal risk to yourself.'

'You played your small part, Warren,' I said handsomely. 'Though it makes you wonder why we took such dire risks – '

It was beginning to work. Lennie put down his book again and turned towards us. 'What dire risks? Listen, the only thing I ask you to do on my behalf is give me half a flaming chance to pass the exam!'

'Which,' I said triumphantly, 'is precisely what we have done, Godber.'

Warren added proudly: 'We're only going to make sure you pass the exam, aren't we?'

Lennie looked from Bunny to me. 'How?' he asked.

I explained carefully: 'By going over the questions with you so you can prepare the appropriate answers.'

Lennie said, with heavy sarcasm: 'In that case, it would be useful to have the appropriate questions, wouldn't it?'

This was the moment. 'You got 'em!' I exclaimed. 'Envelope, please, Bunny.'

I held out my hand and into it Bunny popped the envelope. I then held it out to Lennie who, with a puzzled frown, took it. 'What's this?' he asked.

'Tomorrow's exam paper. Now shift yourself, Len, 'cos we gotta get it back where it come from.'

Lennie said in a curious, low voice: 'The exam paper?' Then, to the consternation of me and Bunny, he flung it down as if it was red hot. 'No!'

We glanced at each other. I asked patiently: 'What do you mean, no?'

'I mean NO! I don't want to cheat. I want to pass this exam honestly.'

'Well, of course you do,' I agreed, realising that diplomacy was going to be needed. 'But honesty is something you can only afford once you've made it. And passing this exam is going to help you make it.'

But Lennie shook his head decisively. 'Don't you understand? I've cheated all me life. That's why I'm where I am. For the first time I want to do something straight.'

I made soothing sounds. 'Course you do. But once you've passed this exam, no one's going to know *how* you passed it.'

Lennie said positively, 'I'll know. Look, if I fail, I fail. But I'm not going to pass through cheating.'

I shook my head sadly. 'Len, Len, listen, will you?

Cheating, my son, is not a crime.' This did not seem to convince him. I bowled on : 'Course it isn't. Cheating is – getting away with it. World of difference. I mean, every-one cheats. Look, the commercial traveller comes home from the smoke to his local branch office. Puts in his expenses : full week's board and lodging at the Savoy, isn't it? But we all know he's been kipping in a Turkish bath in Hounslow.'

Feeling that reinforcements were needed, Bunny took up the task. 'Listen, Len, you know when you play draughts with Fletch and he says he thinks one fell on the floor and could you pick it up, so you bend down only when you straighten up you find the board's re-arranged. That's cheating.'

I nodded sourly. Warren's support was about as use-ful as a rubber ladder but I hadn't much choice. Then, to my indignation, the treacherous nurk turned on me.

'Oh, so you admit it?' he asked nastily.

I waved irritably. 'Name of the game, isn't it? Getting away with it.'

Bunny grinned. 'It's not what you do in life – ' he chanted.

'It's what you're caught doing,' I continued.

'And if you don't get caught – '

'You're away, aintcha? Home and dry.'

But the lad still gave no sign of being won over.

'Listen, Godber,' I tried again, 'you sees a television star, like your favourite, Kojak, Telly Savalas, and you think he's such a great actor. Well, why is he always opening filing cabinets and looking at his shirt cuffs? Why? Because his lines are written up for him all over the place.'

'And that's cheating,' Bunny proclaimed.

'Right,' I agreed. 'But who gives a rats? Listen, son, cheating is only another word for conning. Putting one over. And if that was a crime, the whole country would be doing porridge.'

I picked up the crucial envelope and edged it into Lennie's grasp. To my relief he did not hurl it away again. I pressed on : 'I'll tell you what would be a crime – you turning down this golden opportunity we are handing you.'

Warren said earnestly : 'We took a big risk to get that for you, Len.'

Lennie smiled ruefully. 'All right,' he conceded, 'I appreciate your efforts. You want my thanks? Thanks. But I'll still do it my way.'

And the crazy mixed-up nurk handed me back the bleeding envelope.

I shook my head pityingly. 'If you do it your way, you ain't honest – you're just dumb. Because if you do it your way, you'll fail.'

But Lennie stuck his ground. He said sadly : 'There comes a point when the only person you're cheating is yourself. It's like cheating at patience.'

'Fletch does that, too,' Warren said unhelpfully.

I took him by the arm. 'Come on, Warren, what's the use? Let's leave him.'

Sadly, our efforts despised, we turned to leave. At the door, I paused and turned back. In a mournful voice, I gave the lad some last basic truths.

'You're at the crossroads of life, Godber. You make your own breaks, son, because when you get out there, people are going to give you precious few. You can go up for a job one day with all the qualifications in the world and get pipped by some nurk who's never passed an exam in his life. But he's got the right accent, plays for the local rugby club, and he ain't never been in no nick !'

I dropped the envelope on the floor. Then I turned

and, with Bunny, marched with dignity out of the dell. Only we didn't march very far. Just outside the door we paused. Then we peeped. Lennie stood for a long time, staring down at the envelope. Finally he glanced at the door, nearly spotting me as I jerked back. Then he slowly picked up the envelope. He gazed at it for a moment and started to undo the flap.

The next day, while we were playing draughts, Warren remarked : 'Lennie should be out of his exam soon.'

I chuckled. 'Yeah. I wonder how he got on?'

Warren joined me in the chuckle and, while his head was thrown back, I shifted a piece. I said sternly : 'Mind you, we must never let him know that *we* know the truth.'

'Course not,' muttered Warren, frowning at the board. 'Shtum.'

Warren sighed. Then he rallied and said brightly : 'I knew it would come in handy some day.'

'What?'

'My knowledge.'

I shook my head patronisingly. 'Knowledge in itself, my son, is meaningless. It's how you applies knowledge. Once upon a time some cavemen come up with the idea of a wheel. But he didn't know what to do with it. It was just an idea going "round" in his head.'

I waited expectantly for the laugh but Warren just looked blank. So I sighed and continued : 'The bloke what really cracked it was the bloke who first put one on each corner of a Volkswagen.'

Warren nodded thoughtfully, trying to work it out. While he was thus occupied I flicked a counter on to the floor. 'Oh dear, one's on the floor. Your side, I think, Warren. Could you pick it up for us?'

But a hard light came into his eyes. 'Come off it, Fletch, you must think I'm barmy to fall for that again.'

'What?' I asked innocently.

'You dropped it. You pick it up.'

'How? With my back?'

'Tough.'

I shook my head sadly. 'Gawd, such mistrust in one so young.'

'For once,' declared Bunny, 'I just want to have an honest game.'

He'd outplayed me. Trying to keep my eyes on Bunny and the board, I bent down swiftly and retrieved the counter. Nevertheless, when I rose again the board had an unfamiliar appearance. Warren said smugly: 'Your go then.'

I nodded grimly. 'Is it? Right. Let's see.'

He hadn't been quite as smart as he'd thought. In a lightning swoop I removed all his remaining three pieces. He blinked in amazement.

'How d'you do that?'

'I dunno,' I replied. I wasn't quite sure myself.

But before conflict could erupt, Lennie moseyed into the association area. He seemed relaxed.

'Hello, lads,' he greeted us.

I beamed. 'Oh, Len, son. How did the exam go?'

He shrugged. 'Some questions were a bit tough, but it were not so bad as I thought.'

'No,' I said significantly, 'I'll bet it wasn't.'

He looked thoughtful. 'I was a bit stuck on the Congress of Vienna, but I did well on Wellington's strategy at Waterloo.'

'And we all know what that was, don't we? Put the boot in.'

Lennie smiled. 'I'm going to keep my fingers crossed. But I will admit to being quietly confident.'

I tapped my nose. 'Quietly confident – say no more, lad.'

'Tell you one thing, though,' he said positively, 'pass or fail, at least I have the satisfaction of knowing I did it on me own.'

Now this was on the thick side. I mean, the lad could hardly admit that he'd cheated but he didn't have to be so brazen in his protestations. I couldn't help remarking sharply : 'You what?'

'I did it on me own efforts,' he declared.

Bunny too was outraged. 'Your own efforts?' he repeated incredulously.

I held up a warning hand. 'Er, Godber,' I said tactfully, 'would you like to rephrase that observation. That is, bearing in mind that some of us may know more than you thinks we do?'

But no trace of shame appeared on his youthful face. He said lightly : 'I'm just saying I did it my way. With no help from no one.'

Cheating's one thing but this was dishonest. 'Listen, Godber,' I said earnestly, 'there are many sorts of crimes and we're all here for most of them. But the one thing I can't abide is hypocrisy !'

He never flinched. Looking me straight in the eye, he asked : 'And would *you* like to rephrase that statement, bearing in mind that some of us may know more than what you thinks we do?'

'What?' I challenged him.

Lennie smiled grimly. 'You didn't whip those papers because you cared about my future. You did it because you've got a bet on with half the nick.'

Unlike him, I had the good grace to flinch. But then I rallied : 'Who told you that?'

'No secrets in here.'

I found the answer. 'That bet was an expression of my faith in you.'

'So much faith that you whipped the exam papers.'

'Yes,' I said coldly. 'And which you opened. And don't deny it because we saw you. Which means you certainly qualify for number one in the hypocrisy stakes.'

Bunny said feelingly, 'Worst offence of all in my book.'

Lennie shrugged. 'Yeah, I clocked those papers – but it didn't make no difference.'

'How can he say that?' I appealed to Warren.

'Who actually lifted them?' asked Lennie softly.

'Warren,' I said.

'Well,' suggested Lennie, looking from one to the other of us with a faint smile, 'next time pick someone who can read. He nicked the biology paper.'

And, chuckling softly, the lad strolled away in the direction of our dell.

Final Stretch

Bloke called Harrison. In Maidstone it was – first stretch I ever did. He nicked the key to the stores and locked himself *in*. Since there was no other way out, the screws assumed he was gorging himself in there on tinned peaches and bully beef. Very strong door, naturally, on the stores and it took them some time to break in. When they did, they was amazed to find he hadn't touched a thing. He was just sitting there with his hands pressed to his ears. Turned out that what he was after was simply being alone. He told the Governor it had come over him that if he couldn't be alone, beyond the sight of anyone, for a couple of hours, he'd felt he'd top himself. They treated him decent. Sent him off for psychiatric treatment where he had a trick-cyclist rabbiting at him all day. Never did find out what happened to him. But the point is, I didn't understand it at the time. Now, I do. It comes over you very strong sometimes, the craving for solitude. And never more strongly than at visiting times. Course, at visiting times you don't actually want to be on your tod. You want to be alone with your loved one, beyond the reach of a screw. You wants to forget there's such a thing as cons and warders crowding round you all day long.

Ingrid was saying : 'I know it's only February, but if you book your holiday now it's ever so cheap. So me and Barbara, you don't know Barbara, dad, she's my friend at work – we fancy going to Rimini. That's on the Adriatic. We thought Italy, because your money goes much further there. That's because the lira's the only European

165

currency that's as bad off as the pound. It's either Rimini or Portofino – which is supposed to be rather smart. I believe Rex Harrison goes there.'

I leaned forwards and said in a stage whisper: 'Anyhow, the riot is set for Tuesday. We're going to barricade ourselves in with half a dozen screws as hostages with which we can bargain for better living conditions.'

As I'd suspected would happen, Barrowclough, who'd been hovering at my right shoulder, swung round. I said indignantly to Ingrid: 'I knew he was earwigging.'

'What?'

'Listening to every word he was, of our supposedly private conversation.'

Barrowclough, who'd twigged that he'd been had, protested. 'I was doing no such thing, Fletcher.'

I gave it to him straight. 'Oh yes, you were, Mr Barrowclough. Shouldn't be allowed, hovering.'

He sighed. 'It wouldn't be necessary if we could trust you people not to pass each other contraband.'

'Hear that!' I exclaimed bitterly. I grabbed the packet of cigarettes Ingrid had brought me and suggested: 'Here, check this. There's half a pound of hashish in there!'

And I threw it peevishly towards Barrowclough. As I'd planned it fell short and landed on the floor. He shook his head reprovingly. 'There's no need to take that attitude, Fletcher.'

He stooped to pick up the packet and that gave every visitor in the line a chance to slip contraband across the table to their loved ones. Barrowclough straightened up and handed me back the package. He said haughtily: 'There you are. Now, just carry on.'

'Where was I?' asked Ingrid.

'Rimini or Portofino,' I reminded her.

'Oh yes, well we was thinking of May, before it gets too touristy and – '

I held up a weary hand. 'Listen, girl, has it not occurred to you that it's a bit tactless in front of your old dad? This conversation about foreign climes?'

'Oh.'

'I mean – you know – '

She patted my arm, causing Barrowclough to peer narrowly.

'You've passed the halfway mark, dad. Less to do than's already done. With parole, only another year. Just under.'

'Oh, is that all? That's nothing, just a mere bagatelle, isn't it?'

'Getting rough, is it?'

I smiled wearily. 'Oh, you know me, I'll survive. It's just every time I see you or Marion or Raymond, I realise you're all grown up a bit more. And without me.'

She pointed out : 'I grew up before you come in, Dad.'

I nodded. 'You had, certainly. Grew up too soon, you did. You somehow bypassed puberty.'

'No, I didn't. You bypassed my puberty by going into Maidstone.'

'Doesn't alter the fact that you was wearing a 36D in junior school.'

Ingrid bridled. 'Not my fault – that's nature.'

'Any road – I forewent my parental responsibilities during your most formative years. Same with young Marion.'

Ingrid sniffed. 'Oh, she'll be all right. Don't you worry, Marion will always end up on her own two feet.'

'If she ever gets herself off her back.' But this seemed a bit raw, so I added hastily : 'No, no, I didn't mean that to sound like it did. I mean, she's a lazy little so-and-so. She got a steady job yet?'

'She don't need one, Dad. Her boyfriend Ricky's ever so well off. He's got three cars. He gave her one for Christmas.'

'I'll bet he did.' Some demon prompted me to add : 'Did she get a present as well?'

'Dad!'

'Well –'

'If she marries Ricky, she'll want for nothing.'

'Oh yes? What's he do?'

'He runs these cheap charter aeroplane trips.'

'What's the firm called? Gullible's Travels?'

But Ingrid has never really had a keen sense of humour. She just shook her head. 'No, Sunset Tours. It was him what put me and Barbara on to Rimini.'

'What I'm trying to say is, his three cars was bought from the deposits scraped together by people like you.'

Ingrid shook her head sadly. 'Dad! I hate to hear you talk like this. You never give no one the benefit of the doubt. You're getting so cynical in your old age.'

I said wearily : 'Listen, it ain't no bed of roses in here.'

'You've got nothing to bleat about. You chose to live outside the law, so you accept the consequences. What was it you told young Lennie? If you can't do the time, don't do the crime.'

I was none too pleased to hear my well-chosen words come back at me from my own daughter. 'How d'you know I told young Godber that?'

'He said so in one of his letters.'

I turned and favoured young Godber with a glance of displeasure. But he paid no attention and waved at Ingrid. She waved back.

'So you've been keeping in touch, have you?' I said with some slight edge.

'Only pen pals.'

'Yeah, well, he's going out next week, isn't he?'

'Subject to his parole board.'

'Oh, he'll smarm his way past that lot with his naïve charm, his boyish smile and his one bleeding O level in

Geography. Probably get lost as soon as he's outside the gates.'

'That's why you're so grumpy!' she exclaimed. 'He's going out and you're going to miss him.'

'Miss him? That's not the point. His going out reminds me that I ain't.'

Ingrid gave my hand a squeeze. Barrowclough was mercifully looking in the other direction.

'Won't be too long, dad. Won't be long before you and Mum are going off to somewhere like Rimini.'

I sighed and nodded.

'Yeah, I'd like to think so. 'Cos your mum ain't had an easy life. We never been able to travel, on account of children and incarceration. But now you're all standing on your own two feet, I'd like to make it up to the old gal.'

Ingrid said positively: 'All our mum wants is for you to stay out of trouble.'

'Her and me both, love. This is the last bird I do, don't you worry. And don't tell me you've heard that before, because I know you 'ave. Just that it takes some of us longer to grow up than others.'

Ingrid smiled. She's got a nice smile has Ingrid.

'You've still got a lot of living to do, Dad.'

'Yeah, one of the joys will be catching up on life. Catching up on friends, family, travel – and the repeats of "Upstairs, Downstairs".'

'Tell you what: soon as your release date is set, I'll get in touch with Ricky and he can book you a lovely holiday in the sun.'

'Yeah, well, after Marion and you, why not me and your mum? Then, apart from Raymond, he'll have screwed the whole family.'

So the brief hour passed in fond communing. All too soon it was over and the free ones took wing for the great world while we poor shackled souls trooped back to our dungeons. As I shuffled sadly along I noticed, ahead of me, Lennie deep in conversation with a bruiser called Jarvis. The spectacle did not please me. I was just making a mental note to speak to the lad about keeping bad company when, to my amazement, I saw him suddenly stop and take a swing at the heavy. The next minute they were rolling about near the dustbins.

'Stop that!' called Barrowclough, and that's all I was able to see or hear as the current carried me on towards the old flowery.

I have to rely on Lennie's account for what happened next because I didn't see him again until he slouched into the dell some time later. It seemed MacKay had charged up, bellowing: 'What's all this about then?'

Lennie asked innocently: 'What's all what about, Mr MacKay?'

'Brawling in the yard.'

'We weren't brawling, sir.'

MacKay turned his stern gaze on Jarvis who tried to smile light-heartedly. According to Len it made him look like a wolf with heartburn.

'Just fooling around,' maintained Jarvis. 'Playful high spirits, sir.'

Lennie elaborated. 'We were just re-enacting a big moment from last Sunday's football on the telly. The bit where Peter Shilton dived at Charlie George's feet.'

This delightful picture of innocent frolic did not appear to convince MacKay. He growled: 'I don't recall Charlie George smashing a dustbin lid over Peter Shilton's skull. Not even in the action replay.'

Lennie, slipping out of character somewhat, maintained: 'He would have done if he'd had one handy.'

'Don't be funny with me, Godber.'

'Not trying to be, sir.'

'You two were brawling.'

Lennie shook his head firmly. 'Wasn't, sir, honest. Got me parole board next week. Daft to jeopardise that, wouldn't I?'

MacKay admitted: 'You would indeed, sonny.'

Jarvis had another go. 'Godber's my mate, sir. Him and me are like that.' And he held up two massive digits, lovingly entwined.

MacKay, who hadn't witnessed the affray himself, turned questioningly to his fellow screw. 'Mr Barrowclough?'

'Well,' admitted old Barra, 'I was some distance away, but it did seem to be a vicious altercation.'

Lennie quickly observed: 'Oh, from a distance it could have been misconstrued. But if you'd been close up you could have seen we were smiling.'

He widened his mouth in demonstration. Jarvis did likewise. The effect was unnerving and caused Barrowclough to retreat slightly. MacKay, made of sterner stuff, rounded on the hard man.

'You're no stranger to violence, Jarvis. Your only interest in football was supervising violence at the Stretford End. It's no coincidence that since your imprisonment football hooliganism has declined.'

Jarvis said humbly: 'Didn't know no better then, sir. But thanks to people like Len – '

Lennie supported him. 'It's true, sir. Watch this.' He turned to Jarvis and said firmly: 'Manchester United are rubbish compared to Villa.'

Jarvis swallowed and then returned mildly: 'You could be right, Len.'

Lennie turned triumphantly back to MacKay. 'Doesn't that prove it, sir? It's just that we do sometimes get a bit boisterous in the yard.'

'That's all it is,' insisted Jarvis. 'But to me, sir, Len's family.'

At this moving declaration, Lennie turned to him with quivering chin. 'D'you mean that, Jarvis?'

'Cross me heart.'

'Well, I'm touched. You don't know what that means to me.'

MacKay, who had managed to remain dry-eyed through this performance, sighed and confessed : 'I'm in two minds, Mr Barrowclough. Should I give them solitary confinement or announce their engagement?'

In the end, he did neither, but let them off with a caution. On their way back to the cell block, and when they were out of earshot of authority, Lennie said amicably : 'Got out of that then.'

'Bloody did,' agreed Jarvis.

'Did well in there, us. Abbott and Costello.'

'Morecambe and Wise.'

'We were daft though. Having a go in front of the screws.'

'Should have found somewhere private.'

'We will do,' Lennie promised. 'Because I'm going to punch your lights out, musclehead !'

And with that Lennie turned into his attractive convenience home where I was waiting with an anxious expression.

As soon as I saw him, I burst out : 'I thought I knew you, Godber. What was it all about?'

He sat down and drummed lightly on the table top. 'If someone provokes you, what you supposed to do, back off?'

'If you're up for parole next Monday, most certainly, yes.'

'He made certain remarks.'

'What remarks?'

'Never you mind. Suffice it to say I found them insulting and offensive.'

I shook my head in sorrow. 'If my release was in the balance here, there ain't an insult in the world that would prevent me turning the other cheek.'

'Have to draw the line somewhere.'

'Wrong. You could bring into question the virtue of my old lady, call me a poof, tell me I molest goats – water off a duck's back to me – or off a goat's back, in this case.'

'Perhaps you haven't the same pride as what I do,' he said in a superior way.

'Oh, it's the old pride stakes, is it? The old self-respect?'

He nodded. 'It matters.'

I tried to make him see reason. 'Self-respect is something you preserve on the outside. No such thing inside. When you were sent up you forfeited that. You've ended up just like the rest of them.'

'How?'

'Worried about what they think on the inside. It don't matter. Let me tell you, my son, when you're on the outside, their opinion in here matters naff all.'

He shook his head stubbornly. 'Not doing it for them. Doing it for me.'

I could see I wasn't getting through to him. I tried a different tack.

'I was talking to my daughter today.'

His eyes lit up. 'Ingrid?'

'Yeah, your pen pal. She says, you know, I don't give anyone the benefit of the doubt. Thinks I'm cynical. She's probably right. Know why? Because of people like you.'

Lennie looked puzzled. 'How come?'

'Because if one isn't cynical in this world, one is constantly disappointed by people like you.'

'All right,'' said Lennie with what he clearly thought

173

was irrefutable logic, 'if you're so cynical, why should you give a monkey's about people like me?'

I shook my head wearily. 'Because I had high hopes of people like you. Because people like you could just about make it out there. But – '

'But what?'

'You obviously ain't got the bottle.'

'If I hadn't got no bottle, would I be taking on Jarvis?'

'That ain't bottle – that's stupidity. Tell you what does take bottle in life, knowing when to turn the other cheek. Like Gary Cooper in "High Noon", Alan Ladd in "Shane", er – Gregory Peck in "The Big Country", Glenn Ford in "The Fastest Gun Alive".'

Lennie shrugged. 'Okay, I've seen those pictures.'

'Then you know what I mean.'

'So, tell me something.'

'Gladly.'

'How come those films all ended in the worst fights you ever seen?'

There was undoubtedly some thrust in this observation and it took me a moment to find the correct answer. Then I said firmly: 'I'll tell you why, Sonny Jim. Because Hollywood had to pander to the public's insatiable thirst for senseless violence.'

But Lennie shook his head positively. 'No, you're wrong. Those films raised a moral question, which had to be answered by the last reel. A man has to do – '

'What a man bleeding has to do – yes, yes. Gawd, it's Audie Murphy himself, is it?'

Lennie shrugged. 'There is a basic truth there though.'

'Let me ask you one question.'

'Go on.'

'Would Gary Cooper and all them others have done what they done had they been up for parole next Monday?' This stumped him. I continued: 'And would they have walked into the final shoot-out so willingly had they known their adversary was Reggie Jarvis?'

Lennie said tentatively: 'Alan Ladd stood up to Jack Palance.'

'That was celluloid, not life.'

'It was you brought the subject up in the first place.'

I could see he was weakening. I said sternly, 'Godber, let's have none of your feeble attempts to change the subject.'

'I've forgotten what the subject was.'

But he wasn't wriggling out of it that easy. 'The subject was – is – Reggie, the Red Menace, Jarvis. Listen, Len. There's two sorts of violence inside. One that's born out of frustration and despair, and one that comes from the likes of Reggie Jarvis. Full of Mancunian macho 'cos he's got five years to do and nothing to lose. Now you've got everything to lose. Unless freedom ain't everything. Well then – '

But I still hadn't made any real impression. Stubborn as a mule, that boy, when he wants to be. He said kindly: 'Listen, Fletch, I appreciate your concern, but it's just something that I have to do.'

'I'll make one final appeal to you, Godber. Then I'll wash my hands.'

'Go on then,' he said politely.

'There are three good reasons why you shouldn't take on Jarvis. One, you could jeopardise your parole. Two, it offends civilised sensibilities.' I looked away absently and said no more.

After a moment his curiosity got the better of him. 'All right then,' he asked. 'What about three?'

'He'll bleeding murder you!'

I think it was the next day. We'd finished our stint of backbreaking toil and a few of us were gathered in what we like to think of as 'The Club'. This is a commodious chamber, tastefully furnished with beat-up old tables and benches. Here we indulge in recreational pursuits. Some of us study the daily press to maintain contact with the important social and political issues of the day, such as who won the 3.10 at Redcar. Others prefer mind-stimulating, communal activities such as what Warren and I were engaged upon. He laid down a domino.

'Knock,' I grunted.

Whereupon I sighed deeply and added another match-stick to the kitty. Warren, who was in the midst of a sensational winning streak, laid down another domino.

'Four-five,' he said.

I sighed even deeper, put another match-stick in the kitty and again grunted : 'Knock.'

He laid down another domino. 'Double five.'

I had again to utter the bitter word : 'Knock.'

At which point, providentially, Mr Barrowclough plodded up. He tapped me on the shoulder and said diffidently : 'Excuse me, Fletcher – '

'Oh dear, what a pity. Interruption, Bunny, void game.'

And I threw my dominoes face upwards on the table. Warren seemed less than chuffed by this development.

'Hey ! I only had one to play,' he exclaimed crossly.

'It's hard luck, me old son. But we can hardly continue playing when Mr Barrowclough has something to say, can we ?'

Barrowclough disputed this. 'You needn't have broken up your game, Fletcher.'

'See !' exclaimed Warren.

'Too late now,' I pointed out. 'Showed me hand, ain't I ?'

Warren, with manifest ill-temper, threw down his remaining domino. Barrowclough bent over and studied the battered tiles.

'Oh, you'd have beaten him hollow there, Warren,' he assured Bunny.

'Matter of opinion,' I shrugged. 'So what's the problem then?'

Barrowclough glanced about cautiously. 'Just a word in your ear.'

I eased my left ear, furthest from Bunny, towards him. 'Try this one, if it's a secret.'

But Barrowclough shook his head. 'Oh, Warren's all right. He's a friend, too.'

'Friend of whose?' I asked.

'Godber's.'

'Him and Jarvis – ' the screw said meaningfully.

'What about Godber?'

I sighed. 'What about Jarvis?'

'You know,' insisted Barrowclough.

'Do I?'

'In the yard. After visiting. You were there.'

I played it cool. 'Was I? Where was this then?'

'I must say,' Barrowclough reproached me, 'you're not much of a conversationalist, Fletcher.'

'What you on about, Mr Barrowclough?'

He tried again. 'Something's brewing.'

'Oh, good,' I enthused. 'Two sugars.'

'You know very well what I mean.'

'Do I? Oh good.'

'I'll say no more.'

'Yes, I think you've said enough.'

'As long as we understand each other.'

I nodded. 'Perfectly, Mr Barrowclough.'

He also nodded. 'Good.' Then he glanced about vaguely and ambled off in search of greener pastures.

'What were all that about?' Bunny asked.

I explained. 'Godber and Jarvis had a barney in the yard. No proof, but they know. Want it stopped before it goes any further. If it does, bad for all of us, specially the lad.' I laid down the first of the new batch of dominoes I'd been assembling : 'My down, double six.'

'I didn't hear him say all that.'

'Read between the lines, son. Your go.'

Warren studied the dominoes I'd shoved in his direction. He shook his head incredulously.

'Would you believe it ? I'm knocking.'

'Put one in the kitty.' He did so. I laid down another domino. 'Six two.'

Lennie breezed in.

'Oh, here's Lennie,' Warren exclaimed.

'Hello, Warren. Hello, Fletch,' said the lad cheerfully.

'Never mind him,' I urged Warren. 'Have you got a two ?'

Bunny shook his head. 'No, but it's a void game, isn't it ? Interruption, like.'

And the impudent nurk went to throw down his tiles. I restrained him with an iron grip to the wrist.

'Naff off !'

'But that's what you did when Barra came up.'

'Different, isn't it ? Barra's a screw.'

Lennie pricked up his ears. 'What did he want ?' he asked.

'The topic was senseless violence, the prevention of,' I explained.

Lennie pretended to miss my drift. 'If he wants to stop that, he should get the telly fixed. It's been broken for a week.'

'Jarvis broke that,' Warren contributed.

'Only,' I said judiciously, 'because he couldn't get a good picture. I tried to tell him. I said, if the picture gets blurred, you fix it by adjusting the fine tuner with a delicate turn of the knob. You do not chuck the set against the wall. Mind you, that usually does the trick.'

178

'Can I have a game?' Lennie asked.

'No,' I returned ungraciously.

'Why not?'

'Friendly game, this,' I said with emphasis.

Lennie picked it up. 'What's that supposed to mean?'

'If you was to lose, you might turn nasty, know what I mean?'

'Don't be daft,' Warren protested. 'You know Len.'

'Thought I did. Till this altercation with Jarvis.'

'Change the subject,' hissed Warren out of the corner of his mouth. 'Change the subject.'

'What's wrong with you?' I asked peevishly.

Warren screwed up his mouth even tighter and hissed: 'I said, change the subject.'

I was about to ask him if he was knocking again, when a nasty voice from behind said: 'Godber!'

So that was the reason for Bunny's facial gymnastics. Lennie and I turned.

'Hello, Jarvis,' Lennie said.

'Score to settle, right?' the heavy grunted.

'Any time,' promised the lad.

'Up to you,' maintained Jarvis.

'Ready when you are.'

Jarvis smiled the evil smile of the big gun-fighter confronting the midget farmer. 'What's wrong with now?'

'Why not?' agreed Lennie. 'TV's broke – nothing else to do.'

Bunny gulped audibly and remarked: 'I think I'll go to the lavatory.'

I stood up very deliberately and pressed Bunny down. 'You sit down. Nothing's going to happen, so just hold your horses – or anything else that comes to hand.'

Jarvis frowned at this intrusion, wondering if I might be the local fast gun he'd been hearing about. 'None of your business, Fletch,' he warned.

'It's all our business. A happy nick is a placid nick. Cause a rumpus, you naff it up for all of us.'

'Between him and me,' insisted Jarvis.

'Then, it's between you and me.'

'You don't have to fight my battles, Fletch,' the lad said.

I shrugged. 'No skin off my nose. Few weeks remission won't hurt me.'

Jarvis tried to be reasonable. 'Listen, my gripe's with Godber. But I'll stuff the both of you if you want.'

'Shut your face, toilet mouth,' I said firmly.

Warren leapt like a doe that hears the hounds. 'That reminds me, I really do have to go to the lavatory.'

'I'm going to have you for that, Fletcher,' Jarvis said, and, with disconcerting ease, he picked up a chair.

But I can hold my own. They think I'm slow because I'm a trifle corpulent, and I encourage that belief. But when it's needed I can move. I now moved like a flash to the telly and hoisted it above my head, ready to heave it at Jarvis's ugly mug.

'Everybody freeze!' snarled MacKay, who had popped in unobserved.

Naturally, we froze. 'What's going on in here?' he inquired, unnecessarily I felt.

I explained. 'Oh, we was just trying to fix the telly, Mr MacKay.'

'With the set above your head?'

'Yeah, I was just trying the vertical hold.'

Warren, who had not yet departed for the latrines, gave a startled cry. 'Hey, look – we got a picture.'

I quickly put down the set and the lads all pulled up chairs and began to laugh hysterically at 'The Magic Roundabout'.

After this distasteful incident I took steps to prevent mayhem between Lennie and Jarvis. A couple of days later, I was peacefully darning my almond rocks when Warren moseyed into the penthouse. I glanced at him with displeasure.

'What are you doing here, Bunny? I told you to tag Godber. To never let him out of your sight.'

'It's all right,' the dyslectic felon assured me, 'he's on duty. And Jarvis is in the yard with some of his cronies.'

'Well, we'd better tail Godber when he comes out the cookhouse. Because it's the weekend and this is when it's going to happen, isn't it?'

Bunny sighed. 'I had hoped that you'd have talked Len out of it. If anyone could, you could.'

I shook my head. 'Well, I ain't. Which is a testimony to his pigheadedness.'

'Maybe we should look on the bright side. Maybe the fight won't be tumbled. And maybe Len'll do all right. I mean, he knows a bit. He made the boxing squad.'

I smiled sardonically. 'The boxing squad? Oh yes, the noble art. The Queensbury rules, the fair play and the gumshield. During the time it takes Lenny to proffer his hand for the customary shake, Jarvis will have fractured his groin with his prison-issue boot.'

Warren nodded sadly. 'You're probably right. You can't get odds on Jarvis, because I've tried.'

'Oh, that's charming.'

'Well, fair-dos, Fletch. If there's going to be a fight, and we're powerless to prevent it, it's worth contemplating a flutter.'

There was a certain wisdom in this. 'What odds can you get on Len?'

'Harry Grout's giving a hundred to seven. But I reckon they'll lengthen.'

I nodded. 'I reckon Len will and all by the time Jarvis has finished with him.'

'It's a pity we couldn't get to Jarvis. I mean, if we could put the fix in, we'd make a bloomin' fortune.'

'Fat chance.'

'Could we nobble him? Drugs like?'

'Well, there *is* some animal tranquilliser on the farm. But there's no guarantee it would work on a beast like Jarvis. Not to mention the problem of who sticks a needle in his backside without him noticing.'

Warren tried to be helpful. 'They shoot them into rhinos with blowpipes. I've seen it on the telly.'

I shook my head. 'Subduing a rhinoceros is child's play compared to Jarvis. Anyhow, I think we're getting a bit fanciful, aren't we, Warren?'

'Bit desperate, more like.'

There was gloomy silence for a while. I reached a decision. 'Well then, there's only one thing to be done.'

'What?'

'*I'll* have to take on Jarvis.'

Warren eyed me sceptically. 'You? Do you think you can put Jarvis out of action?'

'No, you nurk. But if I fight him and we're discovered, it's automatically the cooler for twenty-four hours, and he won't come out till Len's passed his parole Monday morning.'

Warren perceived the flaw. 'But hang on, if you're discovered, you'll go to the cooler and all.'

'Yuh, well – ' I shrugged.

'You're going to blot your copy book, Fletch.'

I sighed. 'Yeah, but a few weeks' remission won't do me any harm. But listen, Bunny, I'm going to need your help, 'cos I wouldn't last two minutes with Jarvis. The moment anything happens, you fetch the screws and you better move like greased lightning. Right.'

But Bunny protested. 'Hey, wait a minute, Fletch. If I tip off the screws, that makes me a snitch.'

'If you don't tip them off, son, it could make me a corpse.'

'But, Fletch, think of my reputation.'

'You know the grapevine round here. In two minutes, the true story will be out. That this was a strategic ploy on my behalf, in which you were a vital element.'

Warren considered this doubtfully. 'Well, I don't know –'

'Come on, Warren, naffing hell! I'm the one taking the risk. I'm the one going over the top.'

This reached him. I've always said that, contrary to appearances, there's a streak of humanity in Bunny.

'I'm sorry,' he said humbly. 'You're right, Fletch.'

I stood up. Outside, on Main Street, the bad guys were massing and the time had come when a bloke's got to do what a bloke's got to do. So do not desert me, oh my Bunny, on this my –

'Anything wrong, Fletch?' asked Warren, wondering why I was standing rigid with a faraway look in me eye.

I shook my head. 'He's in the yard then, is he? Come on then, let's get it over with.'

Bunny recoiled slightly. 'Now? Straight away?'

'What's wrong with that?'

'Doesn't give me much time to get a bet on.'

Maybe Bunny is all armpit. Any old how, he accompanied me out into the yard. It didn't take long to spot Jarvis. He and some other thugs were playing pitch and toss. They were about fifty feet away. I set off towards them with a purposeful stride. About five feet away I stopped. I took a deep breath and bellowed :

'Jarvis.'

He turned on the instant – and then smiled affably. 'Oh, hello, Fletch. You want in?'

This was not in the script. Taken aback, I asked feebly : 'What?'

'Want to join in, like?'

I pulled myself together. 'Jarvis. I thought you and me had some unfinished business. From the television room, remember?'

He frowned for a moment but then his face cleared. 'Oh, that? Don't be daft.'

'I meant what I said, Jarvis.'

He shook his head firmly. 'No, you didn't. I know what you were doing – trying to protect the kid.'

With which, the soulless nurk turned back to his game. How would Gary Cooper have handled it? With a definite sense of anti-climax, I called even more fiercely:

'Jarvis!'

But this time he didn't even bother to turn round. He just grunted over his shoulder.

'What?'

'You know when I called you toilet mouth?'

'Yeah?'

'I ain't taking it back.'

That got him. He turned and I felt the adrenalin began to pump into my veins.

'Well, you're right, me old mate. My language is a bit colourful. Me wife's always on at me about it. I try, you know, but I can do sod all about it.'

And he turned back to his infantile pastime. But what he'd said had given me an idea. I said it again:

'Jarvis!'

At last he began to sound a bit peeved.

'Now what?'

'Talking about your wife –'

'Yeah? What about my wife?'

'You're luckier than most of us. I mean, when a bloke's doing a long stretch, you know, his old lady's out looking for nooky, isn't she?'

'Speak for yourself,' he grunted. But at least I had his

full attention at last. I pressed my advantage.

'I am. That's why I'm saying you're luckier than most. I heard your old lady's only been unfaithful to you twice.'

With a distinct sense of triumph, I saw a tiny nerve in his jaw twitch. He asked dangerously : 'Twice?'

I let go with the mortal insult, the one that, in Main Street, would have brought six guns flying out of holsters. 'Yeah, once with the milkman and once with the Household Cavalry.'

I braced myself. The muscle-bound nurk glared. Now, a voice whispered in me head, now he's gonna make his play. Then he threw back his head and laughed.

'That's a good 'un, Fletch. Yeah, that's really a good 'un.'

'Oh Gawd,' was all I had the heart to murmur.

Jarvis's laughter seemed infectious. The other players all joined in, slapping their thighs and wiping away tears. Just about then, a neanderthal con called Crusher, who sometimes does little kindnesses for Harry Grout, strolled by. Jarvis, anxious to exploit the fun to the utmost, called :

'Here, Crusher.'

'What?' called Crusher suspiciously. But he lurched over to the group.

Jarvis grinned at him, chuckled and began : 'Listen to this. I heard that your old lady's only been unfaithful to you twice.'

Jarvis paused for some reaction but Crusher just stared at him impassively. So Jarvis went on : 'Once with the milkman and once with the Household Cavalry.'

There were attentive sniggers from the onlookers. Jarvis, his eyes twinkling merrily, waited for Crusher's response. He had to wait some time, since the big man's nervous system is about as active as an old drainage ditch. But finally the jest reached the ape's vital centres. He frowned and then, with amazing speed, smashed his fist into Jarvis's face. I goggled. A moment later and they were rolling about on the tarmac, pummelling hell out of each other. A moment after that and whistles were blowing as screws converged from all quarters. I raised my eyes gratefully to heaven and murmured :

'All right then, I owe you one.'

Then I strolled innocently away.

I can always recognise Lennie by his footsteps. Thus, a few days later, although my back was to the door, the moment he walked into the dell, I exclaimed :

'Congratulations.'

'What?'

I turned and beamed at him. 'Congratulations. On getting your parole.'

He shook his head in surprise. 'I was just about to tell you.'

'Well, I knows, don't I?'

'How?'

'It pays me to, don't it?'

'But I only left the Board an hour ago.'

'Son, son, I works the admin. block, don't I?'

He nodded. I patted him on the shoulder.

'Anyhow, well done.'

'Thanks, Fletch. Here, the Governor was ever so nice about it. He let me ring my mum.'

'I know.'

Again he blinked in surprise.

'How?'

'I listened in on the extension.'

A faint shadow of reproach appeared on his face. 'Fletch!'

'Well, I wanted to share in your moment of elation.'

Another moment and he shrugged. 'Oh well – '

'She was chuffed, your mum.'

'Quite emotional, really. For her. Wish I could tell me dad – if I only knew where the old bastard was.'

'Well, look at it another way. Your dad's absence meant he never knew you went in in the first place.'

'I suppose so.' His face brightened. 'Came in handy to-day, he did.'

'Oh? How's that?'

'Well, I told the parole board that I thought my father's desertion was a contributory factor towards my temporary diversion from the straight and narrow.'

I nodded approvingly. 'You're learning, ain't you?'

'Thanks to you.'

I lowered my eyes modestly. 'Yuh, well – '

There was a moment of silent communion. Then he said : 'Fletch?'

'What?'

'If it hadn't been for you, I'd have messed this parole up, you know?'

'True.'

'I mean, the fact that you risked solitary confinement and loss of your own remission – well – I mean – well, that's real friendship.'

I said firmly, 'There was no way I was going to jeopardise your parole, son.'

'I realise that now. But I never realised it meant so much to you.'

'Course it did. I had three to one on you getting out.'

Lennie gave this the mental butcher's. Then he shook his head. 'You don't fool me, Fletch. You did that out of the kindness of your heart.'

I shrugged. 'If you believe that, then you are a stupid sentimental nurk.'

But he wasn't put down. 'No, I'm not.'

'Well, you're certainly stupid. As your behaviour over the Jarvis affair demonstrated only too clearly.'

187

He shook his head positively. 'I promise you, Fletch, I did have a reason for reacting like I did.'

'There was no reason in the world worth risking freedom for.'

'Yes, there was. I can tell you now that it's all water under the bridge.'

'All right,' I said. 'Surprise me.'

'You remember when the affray erupted?'

'Vaguely.'

'It was when we was coming out of visiting hour last Saturday.'

'So?'

'Jarvis came up to me and made an obscene remark.'

I shook my head pityingly. 'Oh, dear me! Did that affront your Brummagem sensibilities then?'

'Yes, it did.' Lennie paused for effect. 'Because the remark concerned what he'd like to do to your daughter Ingrid.'

I absorbed this in silence. Then I asked : 'What?'

'I'm telling you this,' Lennie pointed out, 'so you can understand what you presumed was my stupidity.'

I nodded and asked again : 'What did he say about my daughter Ingrid?'

Lennie shrugged. 'Doesn't matter now.'

I contradicted him. 'It matters to me.'

'Best forgotten.'

'I can't forget it if I don't know it, can I?'

Lennie became paternal, which was a nice turnabout. 'Look, Fletch, I've learned my lesson. Thanks to you. Turn the other cheek, right? I've learned that what the Jarvises of this world think matters naff all, because they're animals.'

These were very sound sentiments, being my own, but I found them a mite irritating at that moment. 'All right, all right. I agree with you. I'm not after retaliatory satisfaction. But for the record, just tell me what he said!'

He decided to oblige. 'To put it delicately, he indicated his carnal desires towards her, then reckoned that he fancied his chances, on account of her sexual proclivities.'

I considered this. Then I nodded reasonably. 'Well, she's always had those. Ever since she was thirteen.'

'Anyhow, best forgotten.'

I looked him straight in the face. 'So. You was defending my family's honour, was it?'

'Seemed a good reason. I owe a lot to you, Fletch. I'd never have made the distance without you.'

'Look, don't make me out to be no hero.'

'I wasn't,' he maintained. 'Father figure, maybe.'

But I shook my head sadly. 'I ain't been no great shakes as a dad. In fact, I ain't been no great shakes as anything.'

'You have to me,' Lennie said positively. 'And I won't let you down, Fletch. I ain't coming back.'

I could not restrain a sigh. 'Oh, we all say that. But you'd better bleeding mean it, Godber. You've got your life before you. Out of the last twenty years, I've spent eleven of them doing porridge. That ain't life, that's marking time. I'm not moaning. What's done's done. But it's a terrible waste.'

'I won't be back. Given the breaks.'

'Make the breaks,' I said fiercely. 'No alibis. No if onlys. You can do it. You're not stupid, and you're not evil. You're a good lad.'

He swallowed. This was turning into one of the slushier episodes of *Crossroads*. So I grunted: 'Enough said. Hope you're leaving me your snout?'

'Only right.'

'Chocolate?'

'Fruit and nut.'

'And first thing you do when you get out, you do for me.'

'What?'

'As soon as you get off the train in Birmingham, go straight into a pub and have a pint of best bitter and drink to your old mate.'

'I'm not going to Birmingham. I was thinking of Rimini actually, with a friend. Or perhaps Portofino. We thought May 'cos it's not so touristy then . . .'

'Godber,' I said calmly, meaning to impart to him some sense of mature values, but suddenly the black mist, cleaved by flashes of lightning, closed in. 'Godber, you lay one finger on my Ingrid's proclivities, and I'll flaming kill you!'

It was a few days later. I was stretched comfortably on my bunk, warming myself in the *Sun*, when a chill breeze, immediately recognisable as Mr MacKay, blew into the dell.

'Fletcher?'

'Good afternoon, sir.'

He seemed surprised. 'Good afternoon, sir?'

'Your title, isn't it?'

He nodded and squinted at me. 'True. But I did not expect to hear it so readily from your lips.'

I shrugged. 'Why make waves, eh? Only eight months to do if I keep my nose clean.'

He chuckled. 'Throwing in the towel, are we, Fletcher?'

I was in no mood for banter. I said simply : 'I just want to get home.'

'Yes, I've noticed a certain change in your attitude since laddo's release. Our customary ill-feeling seems to be missing. You seem to have lost a lot of that brash cockney spark. Or are you just acknowledging that the system always wins?'

I shook my head wearily. 'Nobody wins, Mr MacKay.

That's what's so tragic.' And I turned back to the *Sun*.

I thought MacKay had naffed off but a moment later his Hibernian rasp sounded again. 'Normally, I would have hesitated about putting a new sprog in here, Fletcher.'

'Oh yes? Got some company coming in, have I?'

'In the past year, you have not been the healthiest of influences on first-time offenders. But now I don't think I have much to fear. Got a young lad called Nicholson moving in.'

Without lowering the paper, I asked : 'Not a Scot, is he? I mean, we do draw the line somewhere.'

'He's from Sunderland.'

'Dangerously near.'

MacKay said with relish, 'He's a tearaway. Lashes out. Doesn't think. I have a feeling that the new quiescent Fletcher might be just what he needs.'

'Whatever you think, Mr MacKay.'

'So you'll keep an eye on him?'

'Be difficult to ignore him in a room this size.'

'True, but perhaps you'll show him the ropes. Show him what you've learned.'

I lowered the *Sun*. 'What have I learned, Mr MacKay?'

'That there's no point bucking the system.'

'I see. All right, Mr MacKay – sir – I'll watch out for him. I shall simply tell him three things. Bide your time, keep your nose clean, and most important of all – ' and I raised the paper again, blocking out MacKay's evil face ' – don't let the bastards grind you down!'